AN EXCERPT FROM
DANGEROUS CONTROL

"Alice," I whispered. "What do you want?"

"You." She said it without thought, without pause.

Because she didn't understand.

I let out a tortured breath and pressed harder against her, body to body. If we weren't clothed, I'd be inside her. I wouldn't have been able to go for a condom. I would have just thrust inside her and ridden her without mercy. Gentle lovemaking? Fuck. Even with clothes between us, I could feel myself turning to a monster, wanting to devour her, consume her, possess her with rough, unrestrained passion born of too much longing. Years of longing.

My body still tried to argue with my mind, as I pulled her thighs wider and slid my body against hers, mimicking penetration. Maybe she was into violence. Maybe she was into rough sex. Maybe she wanted a monster for a lover. Maybe she was into dungeons where submissive women served Dominant men and weren't allowed safe words.

Maybe...

Maybe I could restrain myself before I revealed the depth of my perversion, and destroyed our friendship for life. I pulled away, exerting the most effort I'd ever exerted in anything, missing her taste before our lips even parted. My whole body trembled at the physical agony of parting our bodies when I wanted her so much.

"Wait," I said. I forced myself off the couch to kneel beside her. "Please, we can't do this. If we start, things will go too far."

"I want them to." She gazed at me, her lips full and kissable. "You can't go too far. I want you, Milo…"

Dangerous Control

Dark Dominance
Book Three

Annabel Joseph

CHAPTER ONE:
MILO

"It's the most wonderful time of the year..."

That's debatable, I thought, as I wove around my parents' massive Christmas tree with a bottle of wine in my hand. Every year, they invited hundreds of celebrities and musicians to a holiday bash at their Chappaqua mansion, and hundreds of people showed up, crowding my parents' second home. I'd hated these annual parties for as long as I could remember, but I'd never missed one. I was giving up a Saturday evening at The Gallery to be here. That was love.

And I loved my parents. Since my brother died of a respiratory illness in our childhood, I'd been their model son, trying to fill the hole my twin had left. Well, most of the time I was their model son. On Saturday nights, I was more of a demon, making my salacious rounds at The Gallery, a BDSM club for those who enjoyed the more serious side of dominance and submission.

"Massimiliano!"

That was my friend Devin using my full name to irritate me. I turned to find him hand in hand with his girlfriend Ella. Fort and Juliet were there too. My two best friends had both settled down into relationships in the same year-and-a-half period. Great for them, not so fun for me.

"Who invited you guys?" I joked as I joined their circle.

"Hey, you got me something. Thanks." Fort lifted the bottle of thousand-dollar Bordeaux from my hand, then promptly handed it back. "Too rich for my tastes, especially since I'm already drunk."

"There's champagne going around." Ella lifted a half-empty glass of bubbly. "Your parents' house is crazy, by the way."

"It's a nice place," I said, an understatement. It was embarrassingly ostentatious, almost as bad as their sprawling estate in Italy, but my friends seemed to be enjoying the party. I wished I were as drunk and happy as they were.

"How've you been, Milo?" asked Juliet. "You've seemed...busy."

"Well, 'tis the season. A lot of people are hoping for violins under the tree."

"Santa's violin elf has been in his workshop." Devin cracked a smile. "Except on Saturday nights. I hear you haven't missed a night at The Gallery in a while."

Ella nudged him. "Shh, people will overhear."

He waved off her concern. "This hoity-toity crowd will assume I'm talking about an art gallery. No offense," he said to Juliet, who worked for an artist-photographer.

"No offense taken," she chirped.

Yeah, they were all drunk. I was about an hour behind, since I'd stopped off for the wine. "I've been to The Gallery every Saturday since..." *Since you guys found love and happiness.*

"Since forever," Fort said, slapping me on the back. "Good for you. We'll get back there one of these days."

Maybe they would, to visit, but they weren't regulars anymore. The occasional drop-in was enough for them, because they were living together, spending time in their home dungeons. No uniforms required, no papers to sign. And I was at The Gallery every single fucking Saturday, because...

Because it was my club, my concept, a place I'd helped build from the ground up. Because I was looking for a new sub, someone to replace my most recent partner, who'd caused too much drama. Because it gave me a safe venue to unleash my sadistic side, and watch others doing the same.

But not tonight, because I was a good son and it was Christmas party weekend. I said goodbye to my friends and wove through crowds of smiling people until I found my parents in a corner of the dining room. They stuck together at these parties, because they were one of those old-fashioned couples who actually loved each other.

"Massimiliano!" My full name was called for the second time, this time by my mother. It wasn't that I didn't like my name, it was just that it had too many syllables for the average non-Italian to pronounce. She hugged me, bottle of wine and all, then passed me over to my father.

"We're so glad you're here," he said, pulling away. "What have you got there?"

I handed over the wine, embellished with a velvet bow. "Merry Christmas, Pop. Thought you could use this in the wine cellar."

He squinted at the bottle, pursed his lips, then smiled. "Beautiful. You didn't have to, but we're glad you did. Aren't we, Luciana?"

"Look at you," my mom said, clinging to my arm. The crowds around them pushed us together. People loved my parents, and my parents loved all people, which was why their parties were so well attended. "Are you still getting taller?" she asked in her thick Italian accent.

"Ma, I'm almost forty."

"Your hair's getting longer, that's for sure." She was teasing. My dark hair had been long forever. "Did you bring anyone tonight?" she asked, a hopeful lilt to her tone.

"No, I'm not really seeing anyone at the moment."

"You know, I think Lala's here. Isn't Lala here?" she asked, prodding my father.

He nodded. "Last I saw, she was over by the Christmas tree."

Had I walked right past her? Thank God. "She goes by Alice now," I muttered. Lilly-Alice Nyquist had been "Lala" from her earliest days, because of her first two initials, and her natural affinity for music. Around the age of thirteen, she'd put her foot down and said she would be Alice from now on, that she'd had enough of being Lala.

No matter her name, I had to stay away from her.

"I didn't know she was in New York," I said.

"She moved here about a month ago. She's playing with the Metropolitan Orchestra, now that her father's retired," said my dad.

Her father, Stefan Nyquist, had been my first serious violin instructor, the one who'd guided me from childish flailing to adolescent confidence over the space of ten years. He was a longtime family friend, and a renowned musician, like his daughter. My parents wished he'd become my father-in-law. They'd pushed me toward Alice for years, refusing to believe it was impossible.

"Maybe I'll run into her later," I said, although I'd do everything in my power to prevent that from happening. I excused myself from the circle around my parents and prowled the outskirts of the crowd in the great room. Christmas classics wafted from my parents' state-of-the-art sound system, and voices rose and fell in merriment, bouncing off the frescoed ceiling.

A waiter stood at the bottom of the wide marble staircase leading to the second floor, holding a tray of glistening champagne with cranberries floating on top. I took one of the flutes as I made my way upstairs.

I loitered in the second floor hallway a while, and the balconies overlooking the great room, saying hello to family and friends. If Lala—Alice—was downstairs, then I'd stay upstairs, and everything would be okay. I took a sip of champagne, tasting tart cranberry on my tongue.

Someone downstairs shouted from the piano. A cheerful group sang carols in multi-part harmony as a distant cousin played, punctuating each line with obnoxious glissandos. It was fun to belong to a musical family, but also loud. My mother corralled groups toward the food tables, and gestured up to me to join them. I would, eventually.

For now, though, I waved and made an escape toward the second floor gallery, a long, narrow chamber of photographs and family memorabilia between the bedroom wings. It had always been my favorite room in this house, which was why I'd suggested "The Gallery" when we were brainstorming names for our BDSM club.

Not that this gallery had much in common with The Gallery where I hurt and fucked masochistic women. This gallery was quiet, with frosted skylights that sparkled in the sun and glowed by the light of the moon. As I shut the door behind me, my gaze went there first, to those skylights I'd stared at since I was a boy.

"Milo?"

The soft, feminine voice sent a chill racing along my nerves. *Danger danger danger.* Alice Nyquist stood on the other side of the room in a fitted ivory sweater dress and tights, smiling her angelic smile. Good God, that smile. Her hair. Her legs. Her tits.

"Milo Fierro! I haven't seen you in so long." She started toward me, half at a run, her arms thrown out in welcome. "Your parents said you'd be here."

I swallowed hard, trying not to shudder as her scent assailed me. "I never miss their Christmas party," I said against her wispy, ginger-blonde hair. "You're the one who never makes it. I was surprised to hear you were in New York."

"I'm here." She pulled back, her wide green eyes shining.

"Look at you," I said softly. "You're here."

"I've been here almost a month now. I would have called you, but I thought you were working in Italy until the spring."

She seemed so pleased with herself, so certain I'd be happy to see her. She didn't understand how hard it was for me to stand beside her, to even be in the same room with her. I'd known Lilly-Alice all through her Lala years. She'd been a rival then, an adversary in pigtails, as likely to laugh as burst into tears. Even though she was six years younger than me, she'd always outplayed me on the violin.

Then she'd grown up and become Alice, the most beautiful woman in the world. Not just the most beautiful, but the most kind, bright, talented, emotional, mysterious, and fascinating woman on earth. I'd been with some top-flight women in my kink career, model-gorgeous women who'd do anything I asked of them sexually, women who'd debase themselves for me at a word.

None of them touched the depth of my feelings for Alice. She was real with me when other women were fake, and from an early age, she'd carved out a special place in my heart. She still played the violin better than me—I'd kept track through the years—but she was also so fucking perfect she made your soul ache.

I rubbed my eyes, nearly sloshing champagne on my sweater. I set the glass down on a table, because I needed my wits about me.

"Not in a drinking mood?" she teased. When she smiled, her Nordic cheekbones made her face look like a heart. Her mouth was so fuckable. *No, Milo. No. This is why you can't be near her.*

I cleared my throat. "What are you doing here? I mean, here in the gallery?"

"I was getting a headache downstairs. Your parents are wonderful, but their friends talk so much. I don't know how they had a son like you."

When I raised a brow, she elaborated. "I mean, you don't talk a lot. You've always been so quiet. Mysterious."

Was she flirting? Didn't she understand that I was dangerous? We were alone in my parents' gallery, so alone. My mind raced, realizing there was no one to stop me from assaulting her, from forcing myself on her and working out all the perverse impulses she sparked in me.

"Does your head still hurt now?" I asked. It took all my self-control not to touch her, not to stroke a finger down her velvet cheek.

"No, I'm fine. It's not that bad. I feel better now that you're here. You look great, Milo, really. You have those..." She gestured, blushing. "Those dark, calming eyes."

Holy shit. If she didn't stop looking at me in that worshipful way, I couldn't be responsible for the things I did to her.

"Why don't we go downstairs?" I said, tearing my gaze from her face. "We'll ask my mom if she has anything for your headache. If you don't take something, it might get worse." I took her arm before she could argue, scooping up my champagne glass in my other hand. "She'll want to fawn over you anyway."

We went down the curving staircase, moved past the glittering tree, and negotiated tables of cookies, cakes, and canapés. I touched the small of her back twice, pretending it was necessary to guide her. I'd forgotten how tall she was, how she could almost meet me eye to eye. It was slightly easier to be close to her with others around us. They could pull me off her if they had to. *She* was safer now, though I felt equally fucked.

"Ma," I said, when we finally found her in the music room. "Alice needs some Tylenol or something. Her head hurts."

"Oh, my dear." My mother cupped Alice's heart-shaped face between her hands and frowned. "Let's see what we can find for you."

We? I had planned to pass her off to my mother and blow this party before my self-restraint snapped. Instead, my mother hooked my arm along with Alice's and dragged both of us to the kitchen. It was as busy as the rest of the house, as the caterer's assistants prepared artistic spreads and the hired waiters refilled trays of champagne. My mother found some ibuprofen and gave it to Alice, along with a tall glass of water. Once she took it, Ma led her to a chair at the long marble counter.

"The headache's not that bad," Alice said as my mother clucked over her. "I'm fine, it's just a little crowded here. I mean, it's a wonderful party. I just haven't been to a lot of them lately."

"Poor dear. It's only going to get more crowded." She turned to me, taking away my champagne glass. "Maybe you should take Lala home."

"She goes by Alice now," I said. "And I've been drinking."

"Pah. A few sips of champagne."

"It's okay," Alice cut in. "I took the train from Manhattan, so I can get home on my own."

"You can't ride back on the train if you're not feeling well. Milo can drive you home," said my mother, offering my services like a shepherd handing a sheep over to a fucking wolf. "Where are you living, dear?"

"In the old Michelin building, near Lincoln Center."

"Why, that's so close to you." Ma grasped my hand, delighted at the coincidence. I tried not to frown. "You were going to leave soon anyway, weren't you?"

She was prodding me to say yes, because she'd raised her Italian son to look after women, especially women like Alice, whom my mother hoped might entice me into a relationship. Her eyes twinkled as she regarded the two of us. Alice started blushing again.

"I guess it's up to Alice," I said, a little surly. "She said she could get home on her own."

"But why should she, when you're here?" My mom patted my arm. "You don't enjoy a lot of noise and conversation either. You too are so similar."

"Okay, Ma." She was only going to get worse the longer we stood here. I turned to Alice, pushing down a sense of dread. An hour back to the city, stuck in my car together. She was so beautiful, so vital and lithe and talented.

Fuck.

CHAPTER TWO:
ALICE

I huddled into the smooth leather passenger seat of Milo's sports car, resisting the urge to hug myself. I'd hoped to run into him at the party, but this was a wildly exciting treat. Milo Fierro, my longtime crush, had just opened the door of his car for me, and invited me into its interior. Then he'd shut the door and walked around the front while I sucked the drool back into my mouth, feeling like a creeper. The older he got, the more attractive he became. He'd always moved through my world with animal grace.

When he got in the other side and looked over at me, I could feel a scarlet blush rising under my skin, because that always happened to me.

"I'm not drunk," he said. "Not even a little."

"I know."

"If I was, I wouldn't drive you."

"I know, it's okay." I stretched my legs, trying to be cool. "I'm only a little buzzed myself. Well, it's mostly wearing off now."

He didn't answer. In fact, he let out a breath that sounded suspiciously close to a sigh as he started his car. The engine roared and settled into a hum, and we pulled away from his family's house, the headlights beaming across the grand front stoop.

Neither of us talked, although it was quiet in the car. Why did I feel shy around Milo, considering I'd known him for as long as I could remember? Probably because I lusted for him, even though he always acted like a distant friend when he was around me. I still fantasized that he was more. Riding in his car—just the two of us, together—would provide masturbation material for months to come.

"So how does it feel, being back in New York?" he asked, finally breaking the silence.

"Awesome." I took a moment to steady myself, so I wouldn't start acting weird or manic. "I mean, I love Stockholm. It's beautiful, clean, all those things, but it's not as big a cultural scene as Manhattan. There's not as much to do, and the New York Metropolitan Orchestra is the best in the world, so when they invited me, I couldn't jump fast enough."

"Makes sense." He shifted gears as we revved onto the main road. "Honestly, I'm surprised it took them so long to come after you."

I made a soft, happy sound, because that was a compliment. I didn't tell him that they'd asked me a couple years ago, when I was embarking on a relationship with a moody Swede I thought might finally chase thoughts of Milo Fierro from my head. He hadn't. None of the men I'd dated in the last ten or so years had come close.

And now I was in the car with the object of my fascination. *Deep breaths. Seriously, don't be weird.*

"It was nice to get the call from Met Orchestra," I said, picking up our conversation's thread. "I'm surprised you don't play for them, or for the Philharmonic."

He shook his head. "I rarely perform anymore. I'm focused on making instruments."

"That's too bad." I studied the lines of his jaw, remembered how handsome it looked with a violin tucked beneath it. "Well, it's great that you're making instruments, but I used to love the way you played."

"I never said I didn't play anymore." He focused intently on the road. "I just can't give up every night to the masses in order to take an orchestra job."

"It's not every night. We have breaks and vacations."

He stayed silent. I wasn't sure if the heightening tension in the car was emanating from him or from me.

"Thanks for driving me home," I said. "I was so ready to leave that party. I mean, not that your parents aren't wonderful." *It's just that I mostly came there to see you.*

"No problem. It's cool that we live so close after all these years."

We merged onto a second parkway and he sped up, his car's engine humming with effortless power. Milo smelled good, like faint cologne, or the varnishes from his violin workshop. Now that I lived in the city, I could ask to visit Fierro Violin's workshops, ask to learn about the process that had created my own beloved Fierro violin.

Of course, Milo hadn't made mine. He was still in his apprenticeship then, working with his father and grandfather. I'd gotten the violin for my seventeenth birthday, which meant Milo had been twenty-three.

At that time, I was sure he was the height of masculinity. My teenage brain would have exploded if I could have seen him now, nearing forty, gruff, virile, accomplished, driving his purring Italian sports car, speaking with his faint Italian accent...

He turned on some music, perhaps to fill the nervous, silent space between us. Classical, of course.

"Prokofiev?" I guessed after a few bars. "Oh, his *Violin Concerto in D.*"

He rewarded me with a smile. "One of my favorites."

"I love it, too." I listened a moment, enjoying the concerto's bright tones, as well as the quality of his car's sound system. "Everyone thinks Stravinsky's so great, with his noisy gimmicks, but give me Prokofiev's playfulness any day."

Milo laughed for the first time that night, really laughed. "Listen to you, Alice. Why aren't you married yet?"

I grinned back at him, buoyed by the music. "Because I've been waiting for you."

"Have you been talking to my mother?" He looked back at the road, shaking his head. "She's been telling me to marry you ever since you turned legal. Crazy, I know. Just because we're both from musical families."

"And our parents are good friends." *And because I've loved you forever, Milo, since I knew what love was.* It was painful for me to joke about us. Not that there was any "us." I bit my lip, holding words inside so nothing ridiculous would burst out, but it didn't work.

"I've always been a little fascinated by you," I said, trying to sound light and airy. "I remember finding reasons to interrupt your lessons with my dad. I almost couldn't stand it, the way you played. You were so much better than everyone else."

"Bullshit. You play better than me. You always have."

"That's not true."

We fell silent as the concerto entered the second movement. Sweeping, harmonious, jumpy, vibrant, the perfect soundtrack for how I felt as we drove south on the Saw Mill River Parkway.

"You always played with more emotion than his other students," I said. "You played like you meant it, rather than playing like mom and dad were forcing you to be there for lessons."

A muscle ticked in his jaw. "Did I?"

Ridiculous modesty. Milo Fierro played like he could lure the angels down from heaven, and he knew it. Horrible, that he didn't perform much anymore.

"I was always so proud of my technique when I was young," I went on. "Until I heard you play, and then I thought my technique was crap, because my eyes didn't burn with fire like yours when I played the hard notes."

He made a low sound, a laugh or a scoff. "That was fear you saw. Nothing else."

"Fear of what?"

"Of not being good enough. Your father was a terrifying teacher. He didn't suffer fools, or lazy students."

"It wasn't fear," I countered in a soft voice. "It was love for the music. You loved playing the violin. I saw it at every lesson, and heard it in every note."

He pressed his lips together. Good. He wasn't going to argue with that. We rode a little while more before he spoke again.

"I don't know what was more important to me in the beginning, Alice. Learning to play the violin, or learning to make one that was good enough to play. Either way, it became an all-consuming relationship for me, learning that instrument frontwards and backwards and inside out. I couldn't make a perfect violin if I couldn't understand how the angles of its body created a sound."

He took a hand off the wheel to sketch a curved shape in the air. Long, elegant fingers, and his deep, resonant voice as he talked about *understanding*. I pressed my legs together, scarily aroused.

"I kind of know what you mean," I said. "About learning it inside out. Sometimes I think of the violin as a heart that's beating."

"Jesus."

He exhaled the word with unexpected force. Had I upset him? I was too afraid to look at him. "What I mean is, I think of my violin as a living thing that I have to nurture and..."

My voice drifted off. I could see his profile reflected in the glass, staring at the road, his dark eyes so intense. I felt the weirdest impulse to burst into tears, thinking about him and his violin, and those Sundays so many years ago, when he'd meet with my father for lessons and sometimes stay for dinner. Those encounters had been so precious to me. Whenever he had to cancel a lesson, whenever he didn't show up, I'd hide in my room and cry. Maybe that was why I felt on the verge of tears now.

"Does your father still teach?" he asked.

"The occasional student. If they're special enough."

Milo laughed. "You have to be special to withstand your father's lessons. I remember him growling at me, pointing out every mistake. *Posture. Tone. What is that grip, Mr. Fierro? Hold your bow with respect or play another instrument. I hear the triangle is nice.*"

"Ha. He was always big on that. *Play something else.* Then there was the whole, *Do you find this funny? The circus needs clowns.*"

"I never heard that one. I was too scared to crack a smile in his presence."

"He loved you, though." I clasped my hands tight in my lap. "I remember that he looked forward to your lessons. He'll be happy to hear that I saw you tonight."

"When you talk to him, tell him I said hello."

"I will."

We stopped talking and listened to Prokofiev as the world whizzed by outside his tinted windows. I wished I'd drunk more champagne, so I could think of more light, fizzy things to say. Everything that came to mind was too stupid, or worshipful, or confessional. *How are you so sexy? You've fascinated me for so long. Are you dating anyone?* I assumed he wasn't, or he would have brought her to the party. Right? Whenever our parents got together, I always listened for Milo gossip, and I'd never heard of him having a serious relationship with anyone.

"Are you doing anything for New Year's?" I asked. If he had a girlfriend, they'd spend New Year's together, and kiss when the ball dropped. My stomach went squirrelly at the thought of him being in love with someone else. It would ruin one of my favorite fantasies, of Milo pulling me into his arms, gazing at me, kissing me until I couldn't breathe.

"I don't know," he said. "I used to hang out with my friends on New Year's Eve, but both of them have coupled up in the past year. Their girlfriends are great, but they only tolerate me."

"I'm sure that's not true." I laughed, partly because I couldn't see any woman *only tolerating* Milo, and partly out of happiness that he sounded unattached. Unfortunately, the laugh that escaped sounded high-pitched and somewhat hysterical. Hopefully, he just assumed I was drunker than I was.

"There's nothing worse than spending New Year's with happy couples," I said.

"Yeah. From now on, I'll spend it at home with my dog."

Invite me to come. We could pound champagne, get really drunk, and tumble into bed to bring in the New Year. I wished for an invitation really, really hard, but he didn't extend one, and we were almost back to Manhattan.

"Are you playing on New Year's Eve with the orchestra?" he asked.

"No, not this year." *I'm totally free that night. Please invite me. You could kiss me when the ball drops. You could do anything you wanted to me.*

But no invitation came, not even a follow-up question about what I was planning to do that night, since I wasn't playing with the orchestra.

He downshifted as we moved off the parkway and into the city. I loved New York, but it always felt claustrophobic after being out in the country, if you could call Chappaqua "country." I looked out the window, trying not to feel wounded by his obvious disinterest in getting closer to me. It was starting to rain.

"What kind of dog do you have?" I asked.

"A rescue greyhound. A black retired racer I call Blue."

"How subversive of you," I joked.

"I try to be subversive." He glanced at me with a quick smile. "I call him Blue because he mopes around. His racing name was Bluebeard, but it doesn't fit him. Do you have any pets?"

"No. I've been moving around too much."

"The traveling virtuosa."

"I'm trying to be more settled," I said, which was the truth. "Now that I have a place, maybe I'll get a low maintenance pet, like a fish or a cactus."

"Hmm. Know your limits."

He was still smiling. I drank it in, enjoying my last moments of Milo, knowing we were almost to my street. We stopped at a light and he pointed to a tall building with a clock tower. "That's where I live."

"The Bridgeport? Wow."

His finger tapped for a moment on the gearshift. "It's a nice building."

"The Michelin's just a few blocks farther, on 63rd."

"I know."

Argh. Give it up, Alice. He's not that into you.

"It's been so great to see you again," I said, preparing myself to say goodbye. "And to listen to beautiful violins." The Prokofiev mixed with the heightening patter of rain outside.

"It's always great to talk to someone who appreciates beautiful violins," he replied. The light turned green. I stared at his knee, and his hand on the gearshift. His strong, masculine fingers made me think of sex. Damn. I wasn't ready to say goodbye.

"Is it true you have a Stradivarius?" I asked.

"Yes."

I squeezed my hands into fists. "Can I see it? If it's not too late? I mean, you already drove me all this way, but now that we're here, I'd love to see it, because I've never seen one." That was a lie. He probably knew it was a lie. My hands were sweating and my legs trembled against the seat.

He looked surprised, maybe wary of my request. A moment later, he flicked on his turn signal. "Okay. Sure."

* * * * *

Milo's apartment was a huge, high-ceilinged altar of masculinity done up in taupe drapes, dark wood fixtures, and deep brown leather couches. My Scandinavian side approved of the lack of clutter, but our apartments had always been lighter and brighter as I was growing up. This wasn't an IKEA apartment. It was a Roman stronghold, all the way.

We took off our shoes by the door, then Milo turned on the lights and walked to the kitchen. "Can I get you something to drink?"

"Maybe. Yes." *Get me drunk. Take me to bed.* I didn't know what to ask for, but it didn't matter, because he reappeared a minute later with a small glass of burgundy wine. Dessert wine? So Italian. I took a sip and gave a soft moan of delight at the sweet, rich flavor. "You're not drinking?" I asked.

"I don't drink and handle the Strad." His dark eyes flicked toward the hallway, then away. "Maybe later."

I heard the click of nails on wood, and a large black greyhound loped into the living room. I put my glass on a side table and moved toward it. "I guess this is Blue?"

Milo lifted a brow. "Yeah. I'm amazed he made an appearance. He's pretty shy."

"He's so handsome." I backed away from the dog so I wouldn't scare him, and sat on the couch. Blue studied me with dark, liquid eyes, pointing his long nose at the floor, then turning toward his owner.

"It's okay." Milo gave his dog's ears a thorough scrub as he spoke to him. "This is my old friend Alice. She's nice."

"What a sweet boy. Can I pet him?"

"Sure, if he'll let you."

I held out a hand and the dog inched toward me, checking me out. He must have decided I was safe, because he lifted his head and came closer, took a prancing step, then jammed his pointed muzzle against my outstretched fingers.

I smoothed my nails over his sleek fur, scratching his ears as Milo had done. "What a beauty you are," I crooned. "You're super fast and strong too, aren't you? You pretend to be shy, but deep inside you're a monster."

Milo laughed. "Monstrously lazy. But he's retired, so he's allowed to be lazy." He watched as I stroked the greyhound's lean shoulders and gently arched spine. "He likes you, Alice. He rarely shows his face when I have visitors, much less lets them pet him."

"I like him, too." I smiled at the dog. "So the feeling is mutual."

"He's not allowed in the instrument room, though."

The Stradivarius. That was my reason for being here. I stood, patting Blue on the head. "Sorry, sweetie. I have to go see this."

I took a last swig of wine and followed Milo down his apartment's central hallway. "This place goes on forever," I said, looking ahead to a far-away glass wall and balcony.

"I bought a whole floor of the building. I like a lot of space, and the open plan means Blue can run up and down when he's feeling frisky. This is the room." He stopped outside a heavy door halfway down the corridor and turned the knob. It opened to a small, dark space that felt a few degrees cooler than the rest of the house.

"It's climate controlled," he said, flipping on a muted light. "Come in and I'll close the door."

I stepped forward, gawking at the cabinets lining the walls. Inside the glass-enclosed structures, there were at least two dozen violins, violas, and cellos of every size and color mounted on pegs, displayed in an artistic arrangement.

"Oh my gosh," I whispered. "This is marvelous."

"I think so. All these instruments are special to me for one reason or another. The way they vibrate, the way they sound, even the curves of their bodies. They inspire me in my work."

As I walked around, taking in the beautiful instruments with their ornate scrolls and richly polished bodies, he moved to a cabinet in the corner, unlocked it, and took out a case. Inside lay a plain, lightly varnished violin. It wasn't the first Strad I'd seen, but it was the oldest. "What year?" I asked, staring at the priceless instrument.

"1682. You can tell the vintage by the color, and the shorter neck. I like that it's one of his earliest ones. They talk about Stradivari's Golden Period, but I'm partial to his beginning instruments. He took more risks then." He held it out to me. "Want to play it?"

"No." I honestly, truly didn't want to. It looked too delicate, too magical. I was afraid I'd break it from pure nerves.

"No?" He gave me a look. "You're the one who wanted to see it."

"I know." I squeezed my hands together, my pulse rushing beneath my palms. "I've been drinking, right? If I did something to it, I'd never forgive myself. You play it, please. You know your instrument better than me."

A smile I could only describe as sensual curved the edges of his lips. "I know her like my own heart."

"She's female?" I asked.

"Of course."

He took a bow from another case—good God, a Peccatte—and sat on a leather-topped stool, propping the violin beneath his chin. There were no other places to sit, so I stood in front and slightly beside him, listening to him pluck and tune for a few seconds. He had a quick ear for tuning. Anyone who made violins for a living had to be highly attuned to sound.

Even during tuning, I could hear the rich tone that Stradivari's instruments were famous for, but when he drew the bow across the strings in the first notes of a lilting Bach piece, my soul rose, perceiving magic.

After the Prokofiev in the car, I'd expected him to play something edgier, or something showy like Monti's *Czardas*, but the Bach was sweet and beautiful. Resonant notes filled the room, lovely and measured, tonally perfect. I stared at him as he played, watched his dark brows rise and fall with the intensity of the music, his lips purse, his black eyes widen during an expressive passage. I watched the tendons move in his neck and fingers, and clasped my hands together to keep from tracing over them.

There were so many things to fetishize: the way he sat astride the stool with his knees splayed, the flawless fit of his suit, the way his hair fell over his collar, with the fabric parted just so. But what I really fell for was the music. He made the bow and the strings sing, and there was that *love*, written so clearly in his features. I felt moisture on my cheek, and reached to touch my face. Milo looked over, his smile fading.

"Are you crying?"

I swallowed and shook my head. "No. Well, a little. It's the way you play." I swiped at another tear before it could fall. "Please, don't stop."

He put the bow to the strings, studying me, and played a few more notes. I don't know what he saw in my eyes. Whatever it was, it was more than I wanted to show him.

"Please don't cry," he said, looking away.

"I'm sorry. It's just you and that violin...and you make violins...and Stradivari made this violin so many years ago... God, there's something about the connectedness of it, and the way music lives on and on and on."

He played a little more, a smile teasing at the edges of his lips. "You've always been so dramatic, Lilly-Alice."

"I know. I'm sorry."

"I like it. I never know what you're going to say." Milo trailed off on a vibrato, lifted the bow and rested the instrument on his knee. "In the car, when you said you thought of your violin as a heart that's beating..." He fixed his eyes on mine, dark and fierce. "It's what I've always thought too, the exact metaphor, and you put it into words."

The hair on my arms rose. "Well, you played like that for my father, like everything was from the heart. You played like that just now."

"It's a Stradivarius. If you're not going to play it with heart, why play it at all?" He handed it to me, forcing it into my trembling fingers when I shook my head.

"I can't. It won't be as beautiful as you. I mean, as the way you played."

I was coming apart and I didn't know why. As I stood there, helpless, Milo guided the violin up under my chin. "Play it, Alice."

"I can't."

"Why not?"

We stared at each other. I'd never been good at hiding my feelings. He had to know I desired him with every cell of my being, and that I was too frightened to play because there was so much longing and meaning in this moment.

"I wish we *could* get married," I said, another renegade tear rolling down my cheek. "I don't want to play your violin. I want to..." *I want to play you. I want your face to look that way because you love me.* "If we got married, I'd be able to hear you play like that anytime I want."

"I'll play for you anytime you want." He touched my cheek to banish the tear before it dropped on the Strad. "You don't have to marry me for that."

My breath caught in my throat, making me give a weird little cough. "But I would marry you, Milo. Don't you think we'd be good together? Your mother would be over the moon." I was pretending to joke, badly. "And our kids would be great at the violin."

I had this image of him showing a child, our child, how to play the violin with his depth of skill and feeling, and I lost it. He stared at me, mute.

"I'm sorry, I don't know why I'm saying this stuff," I said, swiping away another tear. "Maybe the wine. I'm not a good drinker. Forget everything I just said, because I'm stupid."

"You're not stupid. Music makes people emotional, and high-tier instruments—"

"*You* made me emotional," I said, cutting him off. "You, and the way you played."

He looked away again. "Alice..."

"Please take this violin. It scares me."

I gave him the priceless Stradivarius, and he stood to put it away. "Milo," I said when he turned from me. "I do love you. I'm not exaggerating."

"I love you, too." He said it to the cabinet as he arranged the violin in its case and loosened the bow. "I've known you longer than just about every friend in my life."

Every *friend*. He emphasized the word. He wanted me to stop my dramatic nonsense before I embarrassed both of us beyond bearing, but I couldn't stop. Like the Prokofiev in the car, my feelings spilled out, sweeping, jumpy, vibrant. "I would actually, literally marry you tomorrow," I insisted. "I've felt that way since the first day I saw you. I would marry you now, this second, not just because of our parents and our friendship, but for so many things."

He locked the cabinet and turned to me, his expression guarded. "Why are we talking about marriage? I think you've been swept up in the magic of the Stradivarius and Bach."

"Ugh. No. Bach's violin pieces are trash compared to Tchaikovsky or Mozart."

"Holiday magic, then."

I waved a hand, wondering what was in that wine, that a few sips would make me embarrass myself this way. "No, it's the magic of you being so freaking gentlemanly and handsome and talented. Whenever I'm around you, I feel this pull to you, this excitement to be around you."

"Because we've known each other for so long. That's all it is, Lala, excitement because we haven't seen each other in a while."

Lala. The childhood name both thrilled and infuriated me. I knew he meant to push me away with it. His hard, dark gaze gave me nothing. No words, no agreement or disavowal. It just left me flailing in the open, my hyper-emotional words out there, impossible to take back.

"I'm sorry. I always blurt out this crazy stuff." I forced a laugh, flushing hot.

"It's not crazy. We're good friends, and we share an intense love of music. I'm glad you came to see my Strad, and I'm flattered that you were so moved, but it's getting late." I could tell from his tone that he desperately wanted to get rid of me. "I should take you home now," he said, gesturing for me to precede him out of the room.

We walked back down the hallway to his living room, where Blue sprawled in a dog bed beside the giant fireplace. When he saw us, his tail thumped the floor.

"I have to say goodbye to Blue." I broke away from Milo and crossed to his lounging black greyhound. When I crouched in front of him, he extended a narrow paw, half-reclining, lazy and content.

Stroking his fur helped me calm down a little, and get a hold of myself. He eased back down into a sprawl as I scratched his ear, and heaved a sigh of contentment with his tongue half out of his mouth. So what if I'd confessed my crush to Milo? Like, literally told him to his face that I loved him, and wanted to marry him? He had to already know. Yes, the two of us would be uncomfortable around each other forever, now that I'd put it out there. That was my punishment for letting it all spill out, but at least I'd admitted what I'd hidden in my heart for so long.

"I'm sorry I made things weird between us," I said, turning and getting to my feet. "You know how I am."

"Yes. I know."

He'd come closer while I was petting Blue. One hand was thrust in his pocket, and I couldn't read the somber expression on his face. Then the hand was out of his pocket, moving toward me, cradling my chin. His other arm came around me, pulling me against his long, hard frame. I gasped as he tilted my head back and pressed his lips to mine.

CHAPTER THREE:
MILO

I held her harder than I meant to. She was so delicate, so warm, so full of life and emotions. I didn't mean to kiss her. Damn it, I wasn't supposed to kiss her. I wasn't even supposed to have her at my place. Weakness, to put on that turn signal and bring her here where we could be alone together.

But oh, how many fucking times had I dreamed about kissing Lilly-Alice Nyquist? How many times had I imagined the curves of her body beneath my fingers, the heat and taste of her mouth? Subtle notes of port wine and longing. Fucking *love*. She'd hit the nail on the head with that word.

"No," I murmured against her lips, at the same time I pushed her against the doorjamb to trap her in my grip. She responded to my force with trusting surrender, because she didn't understand the danger she was in. Sweet, tantalizing Alice, with her blushing, breathless declarations of love. She wanted to marry me? She had no idea how much I enjoyed hurting women, making them cry. I was a man who prized sexual obedience and surrender. Even if I explained what I was into, even if I paused our kiss and told her everything right now, she wouldn't understand.

My hands moved over her body, exploring the curves beneath her soft, embroidered sweater dress. I reached under her hem, pushing up the skirt just enough to cup her ass and slide a fingertip along the outline of her panties. I found bare skin, smooth and warm. Her tight little butt cheeks begged to be squeezed and parted, so I could plunder her innocent asshole with my raging erection.

Jesus, really? That's the first place your mind goes?

No, I couldn't do this. Even now, she was leaning into me with unwavering trust. *Stop. Stop now, before you do something you can't take back.* My mind raged at me to stop, but my body couldn't hold her close enough. I couldn't kiss her deeply enough. I found myself groping her, grasping one thigh, practically carrying her over to the couch.

Then I was on top, and she was under me. I pulled down the hem of her dress, covering her panties and upper thighs, like that would stop me from going too far. When she parted her legs, I groaned and lifted onto my elbows, because if our bodies came together that way, cock to mons, I would tear off the clothes between us and ravage her.

I think my groan finally clued her to the danger. She stopped trying to pull me close and looked into my eyes instead, twining her fingers in my hair. I kissed her, trying to be tender, but going rabid and wild within moments, because she was too damn alluring, and I'd wanted to kiss her lips for so long.

Yes, and you didn't, because you can't do this. You have to stop this.

I kissed her harder to silence the voices, and made fists to prevent myself from grabbing her hands and pinning her down. Our legs were entwined, though, and she was arching against me, making needful sounds.

Shit. Maybe I could give her what she needed, as a service. I was a Dominant, but maybe I could serve, just this once, and put her needs before mine. Maybe I could quiet the violent spirits that wanted to possess her, and make gentle love to her instead, the way a normal, considerate man would. How hard could it be? I could go through the motions. I could do it without hurting her. Maybe.

I let my body ease down against hers. Her arms came around me, holding me close, making me shudder with the depth of longing to be inside her. I slid along her body so my rigid cock lay against her center, with only our clothes between us. I knew she could feel my hard-on through my pants, but its size and breadth didn't seem to faze her. She pressed her body to mine, all her slender muscles taut with desire.

"Alice," I whispered. "What do you want?"

"You." She said it without thought, without pause.

Because she didn't understand.

I let out a tortured breath and pressed harder against her, body to body. If we weren't clothed, I'd be inside her. I wouldn't have been able to go for a condom. I would have just thrust inside her and ridden her without mercy. Gentle lovemaking? Fuck. Even with clothes between us, I could feel myself turning to a monster, wanting to devour her, consume her, possess her with rough, unrestrained passion born of too much longing. Years of longing.

My body still tried to argue with my mind, as I pulled her thighs wider and slid my body against hers, mimicking penetration. Maybe she was into violence. Maybe she was into rough sex. Maybe she wanted a monster for a lover. Maybe she was into dungeons where submissive women served Dominant men and weren't allowed safe words.

Maybe...

Maybe I could restrain myself before I revealed the depth of my perversion, and destroyed our friendship for life. I pulled away, exerting the most effort I'd ever exerted in anything, missing her taste before our lips even parted. My whole body trembled at the physical agony of parting our bodies when I wanted her so much.

"Wait," I said. I forced myself off the couch to kneel beside her. "Please, we can't do this. If we start, things will go too far."

"I want them to." She gazed at me, her lips full and kissable. "You can't go too far. I want you, Milo. I want to kiss you and make out with you. I've wanted that forever, and if you want to go to bed together, that's okay too. I'm not a virgin." She laughed, a tight, scared laugh. "I'm not saving myself for marriage or anything."

Go to bed together. That was how she put it. I stroked a lock of her hair, hating that I was this person, this deviant who didn't dare *go to bed together* with someone I treasured so much. "You don't understand. I—I can't."

She sat up, pulling her dress's hem a little lower. "Why? Are you seeing someone else?" She looked embarrassed. Sad. "I thought you were single."

"I am. It's just..." I rubbed my eyes and let out a groan, willing my erection to subside. "I can't do this because I respect you too much."

"Oh God. You *respect* me." Her head fell back against my couch. "I'm throwing myself at you, and you're not interested."

"Alice—"

"It's okay."

She stood, and I stood too, catching her before she could back away. She was upset, and I could barely think. I wanted her, still. I wanted her so hard and so rough, so violently that it would feel like rape to her, even if it was consensual.

I had to get her out of here, but now she was crying. I took her in my arms, trying not to stab her with my granite-hard cock.

"This is awful," she said, shedding tears against my shoulder. "I'm so sorry."

"Why are you sorry?" The last thing she should have been was sorry. I was the monster.

"I came here to do this. I mean, a little bit, I asked to see your violin because I wanted to—" She burst into more tears, sniffling through her confession. "I thought, maybe, the two of us could have something, you know, more than a friendship."

"Alice, listen." I tilted her head up so she had to meet my gaze. "We will always have a friendship."

She gave a wild, broken laugh. "You're so wonderful to say that. This is just really embarrassing, you know?" She pulled away from me, shaking her hands like she was shaking off everything that had just happened between us. "But I get it. You want a friendship only. That's okay."

She thought all of this was a rejection. She thought there was something lacking in her that made me pull away. I could see it on her face, plain as a printed book, and it was so far from the truth I wanted to laugh.

I couldn't let her go on believing that. What could I tell her, to explain but not really explain? If I told her the full and honest truth—*I want to hold you down and hurt you for my sexual satisfaction*—it would only make things worse.

I told a half-truth instead. "Things are complicated with me right now."

"You don't want a relationship." It wasn't a question. She said it matter-of-factly. "You just want sex. Is that what you're trying to say?"

"No. Why would you think that?"

Her gaze dropped to my crotch, where my pants did a damn shitty job of hiding my lingering erection. "You got excited," she pointed out, "so you can't have no feelings for me at all."

"Men get excited when—" My voice cut off. It was even worse to make her think any female body could elicit the reaction she got out of me. "Okay, yes. It excited me to...to see that side of you come out when I kissed you. The sensual side. It was beautiful to see you so aroused, and I was...God, Alice...I got aroused too. But you have to understand that I'm just not...not in a position where I can..."

"Please stop trying to explain," she said.

I fell silent, grateful, because every word felt like a lie, and I was too cowardly to tell her the truth. Blue watched us moodily from his bed by the fire.

Damn it all, I thought. *I want you so badly. If you knew...* But I couldn't tell her. I bit the inside of my lip to keep the words inside.

"Okay, you know what?" She took a deep breath and faced me. "I just want..." She put her hands together in front of her lips. "I want to put all this weirdness behind us. I don't want you to avoid me, or run away from me at your parents' future parties."

"I wouldn't. I won't."

"We have to stay friends, because I want you to teach my kids how to play the violin some day. You know, if I ever have kids."

I forced the tension in my nerves to unfurl. Alice could make everything okay. She'd always been the emotionally gifted one. "If you have kids, I'll teach them the violin," I agreed.

She laughed, a mostly natural laugh that signaled the worst had passed. "You should see your face, Milo. All you want right now is to get away from me."

All I want right now is to tie you to my bed and ravish you in quasi-legal ways, but whatever... "That's not true," I said aloud. "I don't want to get away from you."

"Can I sleep over tonight, then? It's cold, and I feel too tired to go home." She glanced over at Blue. "Maybe he'll let me share his bed."

I sighed inwardly. I could let her sleep in my guest room, easily, but then she'd be close, too close, and I'd obsess about her all night. But I couldn't say *no, you can't stay*, after just denying that I wanted to get away from her. I had to make it so we could stay friends.

Blue appeared and nuzzled her hand, then mine, looking up at me as if to ask, *What the fuck is wrong with you? Put her in the guest room, dude. What's the worst that can happen?*

"Of course you can stay over," I said, ignoring Blue's judgmental gaze. "Maybe we can get up and go to breakfast in the morning."

Because that was the kind of shit friends did. I needed her in my life, even if her closeness threatened my sanity and self-control.

* * * * *

I didn't think I'd be able to sleep at all with Alice in the guest room, considering it was just down the hall from my sex dungeon, but I did, drifting in and out of sensual dreams. I finally fell into a deeper sleep around five or six in the morning. It lasted until ten, when I woke to a silent apartment, and a small note propped against the pillow beside me.

Milo,

I'm so embarrassed about the way I acted last night. I shouldn't have opened the box on all my crazy feelings, because I knew you didn't want me to. I did it anyway, and I regret the discomfort I caused. I'm heading home so you don't also have to deal with an awkward breakfast.

Still, thanks for showing me your Strad, and for kissing me. You're really good at it. (Both things. Playing the Strad and kissing.)

Your friend,

Alice

I looked around my bedroom, alarmed that I'd slept so late. I didn't have to be anywhere, I was just upset that I'd slept through her exit. How had she gotten home? Had she walked to the Michelin building alone in the early morning darkness? I didn't have her phone number to check that she got home all right. Damn it.

I needed some coffee. I headed toward the kitchen, then heard a soft snort from Blue. He was lying on the sofa nearest the fireplace, cuddling as well as he could against Alice's reclining form. She'd pulled a blanket over herself, and slept with one arm tossed above her head. The other rested on Blue's back.

34

So she hadn't made it home yet. Good. She looked so comfortable on my couch with my dog, so cute and domestic. So sweet.

Too sweet.

While the coffee brewed, I picked up my phone from where I'd tossed it on the counter. As soon as I checked it, it rang, flashing my father's number. I sent his call to voicemail, but one ring was enough to wake Alice. She blinked at me in the daylight sun, confused for a moment.

"Good morning," I said.

"Good morning. I didn't leave after all."

"I see that."

She ran her hand up Blue's back. "He wouldn't let me go out the door. Well, he didn't want me to leave, and I was afraid he'd bark and wake you up."

I fiddled with the coffee machine to hide my nerves. She was still here. We'd kissed. Things definitely still felt awkward. "Coffee?" I asked.

"Thanks. That sounds good."

"Cream and sugar?"

"Just sugar."

I could feel her eyes on me as I poured coffee into mugs and doctored hers with some sugar packets I kept around for my mom. "You didn't have to sleep on the couch," I said, stirring her drink.

"I intended to slink out of here before you woke up. That was a fail."

"Awkward breakfasts are underrated." I carried her coffee over and met her eyes, so she'd know everything would be okay. "There's a great breakfast place downstairs on the corner. Blue, you wanna go out, boy?"

My dog detached himself from Alice's side with a luxurious stretch and yawn, and followed me down the hall to his fake lawn on the back balcony. It was cold, so Blue did his business quickly, then skittered back inside, ready to eat breakfast and sleep for a few more hours. Alice curled on the couch while I fed Blue and changed his water. She drew her blanket around her like a shield, looking as disheveled as I felt.

"Oh, your phone rang while you were outside," she said.

35

I checked the screen. My dad again. Whatever he wanted, it would have to wait, because I had no idea what to do with Alice now that daylight had come. Take her to breakfast, obviously. But what to say then, when we were facing each other across a table? Last night had happened, and neither of us would forget it, not for a while.

"It's okay," she said, as I looked at her in ponderous silence. "I get it. I understand."

"What do you understand?"

"The friendship thing." She shrugged. "I thought about it last night, and I get the reason you can't see us surviving as a couple. You've known me too long. You knew me when I was immature and annoying." She made a face. "Maybe I still annoy you."

"You don't annoy me." I went to sit on the other sofa, near her, but not too near. "I hate to say something so stupid and worn out, but...it's not you. It's me. I wouldn't be good for you." That was true. I was being honest with her now. "I feel connected to you, Alice, in a pure and long-standing way, and I don't want to ruin the history we share by exposing you to the relationship Milo, who's really an asshole."

"You seem pretty easy to get along with most of the time. I guess I don't know you, not the way I think."

She was skeptical. She thought I was bullshitting her. *Fix this*, I berated myself.

"I love you as a friend and I always will," I said, and I meant it intensely. "But a relationship between us, a romantic relationship... Well, it would be a disaster."

She sighed, looking down into her cup, and then gave a little laugh. "You've said that same thing, more or less, at least half a dozen times in the last twelve hours. I guess I have no choice but to believe you."

"You must have tons of men pursuing you. You can't be that hard up."

"Hard up? Wanting you is 'hard up'?" She shook her head. "Whatever. To answer your question, I'm pretty picky when it comes to men. There've been a few who seemed promising, but they always disappoint me."

Because you're perfect and lovely, and newsflash, I'd disappoint you too. Or horrify you. Or both.

My phone rang again, my dad calling for the third time in fifteen minutes. "I'd better take this," I said, swiping to pick up. "Hi, Pop. What's going on?"

My father's voice sounded rough. "I'm calling about Lala. Alice."

My mother grabbed the phone, her voice loud and hysterical. "They can't find her, and she's not answering her phone."

My dad broke in. "There was an explosion. They've called and called her cell and she's not answering."

"Ah, Massimiliano!" I could tell by her voice that my mother was crying. "We were afraid for you too, because you took her home."

"Wait, Ma. What? What kind of explosion? When?"

"Early morning hours, the whole Michelin building, and half the building next door. Stefan and Freja called us because they can't reach her. They want you to go check..." Her high-pitched voice dissolved into a fit of sobs, and my father took back the phone.

"There was an explosion," he said. "A gas line, early this morning. Half the building was blown away, and the other half caught fire. They can't find her, Milo. No one can find her among the...among the casualties."

"Papa, stop. Alice is okay. She's here right now, sitting on my couch." In fact, she was staring at me, wide eyed. My mind reeled. An explosion early this morning? Holy fuck. "She slept here last night, Pop. In my guest room," I added, because they were Catholic, and those things mattered even when you were recently afraid someone might be dead.

Alice mouthed, "Is everything okay?"

I didn't know how to answer that. On the phone, my parents both sounded like they were crying now. "She's there?" my mother sobbed. "Lala is there with you?"

"Yes. She came up last night to see my Stradivarius. We started talking and it got so late, she slept in the guest room rather than go home. We're just having coffee. She's right here."

On the other end of the line, my emotionally stressed parents repeated *oh my God*, *Praise God*, and *Thank you, God* several times, although it had been Blue, not God, who stopped her from going back to her apartment where she might have been…

Holy Christ. Where she might have been killed in a gas explosion early this morning. It hit me, and I rested a hand on Blue's head. "Thank God," I said, just like my parents. "Thank God you wouldn't let her go home, buddy."

"Keep her there, Milo," said my father. "And don't turn on the news where she can see. It's a terrible scene. She'll be upset."

"Take care of that girl," my mother yelled.

"I have to hang up and call the Nyquists," my father said, talking over her. "Tell Lala to call her parents too, they're hysterical." With one last *Thank you, God*, he ended the call.

"What was that about?" she asked.

I looked at her, dazed. "There was a gas explosion this morning at your building. Your parents couldn't reach you, and they didn't know where you were."

"What?"

"An explosion. Some gas line problem, I guess, and a fire. Everyone was in a panic because they couldn't reach you."

She grabbed her phone. "Shit. It died last night, and I didn't have my charger."

"Don't worry, my parents are calling your parents. Give me your phone. I'll charge it." She held it out, her fingers shaking. "You can call them from my phone when you're ready, so you can let them know you're okay."

Here we were, fucking around with our phones and chargers when she'd almost fucking *died*. I left her phone on the counter and took her mug as she sat frozen in place. "An explosion," she said to herself. "My apartment?"

I sat beside her. "The Michelin building. I think it must have been pretty bad."

"But we didn't hear anything. Wouldn't we have heard it? I live just a few blocks away."

Did she want me to tell her it was all a mistake? That it probably hadn't happened after all? My parents' hysteria said otherwise. "I'm sorry. Do you want me to find more information? We can look online."

"Oh no," she cried, covering her face. "Oh no, oh no."

I put an arm around her, wanting to offer comfort, but how did you comfort someone who'd just lost her home and everything in it? "I'm so sorry," I said. "But thank God you weren't there. If Blue hadn't kept you here..."

She shook her head. "I can't... I can't..."

"Take a deep breath. Everything's going to be okay. I'm so sorry, Alice." I pulled her closer as she dissolved in tears. "Things are replaceable," I said gently.

"Not everything! My violin," she sobbed. "My Grapeleaf. My Fierro." She gazed at me, her wet eyes tormented. "It was my own beating heart."

She turned her face into my chest. I held her, stroking her hair. "It's going to be okay. The Fierro is replaceable."

"No, it's not replaceable. Not that one. I loved it. It was perfect for me. I'll never find another one like it."

I hugged her, offering silent support as she trembled and cried for her lost instrument. To a musician at her level, it was an indescribable loss. Her "Grapeleaf" Fierro had been made by my father, with special care for his best friend's daughter. He'd crafted an instrument for a prodigy, a violin that could be passed from her and her family to musicians and collectors hundreds of years into the future, to become their heart.

I remembered when my father gave it to her on her seventeenth birthday. I remembered it vividly, because I'd done secret work on that violin, etching a heart into the back of the body, curving the edges so it would blend in with the maple as I varnished it. Varnishing was all my father trusted me with at that stage. *It will make it sound better*, I told myself, scratching the infinitesimal curves like a shaman casting a spell.

Somehow, he never noticed the heart, although I could pick it out from any distance. Alice didn't notice it either, not in the uproar of applause and congratulations at her party. I remembered the trembling, reverent way she'd accepted the violin from my pop. She'd played it for all of us, her eyes shining with tears. My father had known, as any good maker knows, how to craft a violin that would complete her, and I'd put my spell on it too.

Now it was gone. There'd been an explosion, and my handiwork was gone, along with her musical heart, and nearly, her life.

"You should call your parents," I said, after she'd cried enough to wet my tee shirt. "They'll need to hear your voice."

* * * * *

My mom and dad arrived from Chappaqua within the hour, bringing clothes, coats, and shoes from my mother's closet, even though she was shorter than Alice.

"Everything will be all right," my mother assured her, over and over. "You poor girl."

I was glad she was there, taking charge. I used Blue as an excuse to go out on my balcony to collect myself. I felt numb, encased in unresolved feelings. I was anxious and sad for Alice, and freaked out at what might have been, but I also kept thinking about last night's makeout session, which seemed extremely crass under the circumstances. I thought about the warmth of her body against mine, the way it felt so perfect and

40

necessary. I remembered kissing her, a kiss that had simmered for untold years, then caught fire in five reckless minutes before I regained control.

No, I couldn't think about fire. I stroked Blue's smooth fur to keep him warm, and waited in the wind for my hands to stop shaking. My cheeks grew irritated by the winter air.

"Let's go back in," I told Blue, and he traipsed down the hall before me, energized by his foray outside. He went right to Alice, shoving his muzzle into her welcoming embrace.

"What a cold nose you have," she said, petting him. Her voice was thick from crying. "And what a good dog you are, bud. Thanks for making me stay."

While she gazed at Blue, my mother and father started a fierce conversation in Italian, softly, under their breath. They were arguing about where Alice would go, whom she should live with until she found another place. They lived too far away for her to be able to commute to the city, and having just moved here, Alice didn't have any friends she knew well enough to move in with.

"The building's insurance," I said in Italian, interrupting their whispered fretting. "They'll find her a temporary place to live."

"When?" my mother replied. "It's the holidays. And where? A hotel in a bad part of town?"

"I don't know, Ma. I don't know how it works."

We paused and looked at Alice, curled in the corner of my couch, her head held high, but her eyes closed.

"She might as well stay here," said my father, in English.

My mother frowned at him, and they were off in Italian again. "Look at her," said my dad. "She's tired and traumatized. She needs his protection."

"But they're not married."

"Don't you think your son can be trusted? She's an old family friend."

My mother waved her hands in alarm. "And I want it to stay that way. What will Stefan and Freja think?"

"They'll be grateful she's taken care of. If you must play chaperone, you can move in with Milo and Alice until she finds another place."

I raised my voice over their clipped conversation. "You should speak English in front of Alice." I crossed to the couch and sat beside her. The numbness persisted, the urge to be businesslike and take care of things. It allowed me to shove aside the fact that it would be excruciating to have her stay with me, constant temptation within reach. "They're wondering where you're going to stay," I said gently. "They want you to feel safe."

She looked shocked, like she hadn't even thought about that yet. "I...I don't know."

"You can get a hotel room if you'd like, something close to your work. Your insurance company should give you a stipend when your claim goes through. You could stay with my parents, if you don't mind commuting from Chappaqua, or you could stay here for a while, in the guest room." Jesus, if my parents knew that we'd made out on this same couch last night...

"If you don't feel comfortable with that, we can find you something else," my mother said quickly.

"But you would be safe here," my father said with equal fervor. "Milo could look after you. You've had a difficult time."

"But if you feel it's not appropriate..." My mother, who'd been trying for years to engineer our wedding, got cold feet at the idea of emergency cohabitation. I loved my parents, but they were making a bad situation even worse.

"Live here," I said. "At least until you're back on your feet again. I have plenty of room, and Blue loves you. My parents are just worried we'll be unable to control our physical urges while we're cooped up in this apartment together without any supervision."

"Massimiliano," my mother chided. "That wasn't what I said."

"It's what you implied."

I saw the first shadow of a smile on Alice's drawn features. "It's okay, Mrs. Fierro. Milo and I are just friends. We have no romantic interest in each other, honestly." She said it with an edge of resignation. My parents probably didn't hear it, but I did. She turned to me, and I saw how exhausted she was by everything. "If you don't mind me staying here, that would be great."

"I don't mind at all."

I said it quickly, and I meant it. The rest of my bullshit was secondary. My lust, my longing, I'd learn to overcome it.

"Hopefully it won't take that long to find another place," she said.

"It doesn't matter. You can stay as long as you like." I said this in a carefully modulated voice, even though my numbness was starting to wear off.

Shortly afterward, while my parents sat with her, I put on a coat and walked the three blocks to the Michelin building, or what was left of it. I wasn't sure what I hoped to find there. Maybe a mostly-intact violin case lying in the gutter across the street, blown from her apartment's window to safety. What I found was absolute destruction, a building reduced to rubble, and bricks melted by the magnitude of the fire that followed.

Fuck. Everything was gone. I'd hoped I'd find something to take back to her, some small thing that had survived, that was miraculously hers, but there was nothing but brick, metal, and ash strewn in the street, surrounded by a plastic security boundary. *Danger. Do Not Cross.*

I stared at the hole where her building had been, glad she wasn't with me to see it. It was sad to lose the Grapeleaf violin, but if I'd taken her home when I'd wanted to...or if Blue had let her leave in the middle of the night...

If the world had lost both of them at once, Alice and the violin, I don't think I could have lived with the tragedy. I kicked a scorched brick lying near my foot, imagining what might have been, and turned on my heel to walk away.

CHAPTER FOUR:
ALICE

Snow fell outside, a late December storm obscuring the holiday lights still blinking in the city. I curled in my bedroom's shallow window seat, toying with the hem of a pale green sweater Milo had brought me the day before. He called them "presents," and he bought me too much, but I didn't feel strong enough to go out and buy a whole new wardrobe, so his kindness was appreciated. Christmas had passed without much merriment, bringing useful gifts and necessities. It was one of the few days in the last week that I got out of bed.

Now New Year's was a couple days away, but I wasn't feeling very festive. I no longer fantasized about swooning in Milo's arms as we rang in the New Year as a couple. We weren't a couple, and we never would be. We were just friends.

Blue stirred, nudging me with one narrow paw, letting me know the other member of our pack was home. He somehow knew the moment

Milo stepped on the elevator down in the lobby. "Thanks, bud," I said, scratching one of his ears. "How do I look? Slovenly? Maybe I should at least brush my teeth."

I'd been officially living at Milo's house for a week, and I wasn't a great roommate. I slept weird hours, ate all the Christmas cookies his mother brought us, and stole his dog's affections so he'd keep me warm in bed. Well, Milo wasn't going to do it, although he made sure to check in with me a few times a day. *How are you feeling? Is there anything I can do? Is the bed comfortable?*

If the bed wasn't comfortable, I wouldn't have stayed curled up in it for fifteen hours at a stretch. It was a luxurious, king size bed in a minimal but beautiful guest room, with fluffy blue blankets and sheets. The ivory carpet cradled my feet in softness when I managed to haul myself out from under the covers. The whole room was like a den of coziness, and I was so grateful for it. I needed it to keep everything at bay, from the loss of all my worldly possessions, to Milo's rejection of me as anything but a friend. One was more life-altering than the other, but both really sucked.

I was dressed, at least. I washed my face and brushed my teeth, and felt more presentable. Blue's yawn and the soft, rumpled sheets beckoned me back to the bed, and I picked out a book from the nightstand so it would look like I did more than sleep. When Milo knocked, I pretended to be engrossed in a JFK biography as I invited him in.

"Hi, Alice," he said. "How are you doing?"

I peered at him over the book. He was in a dark gray sweater that accentuated his biceps, and jeans that accentuated...everything. He was holding a couple of department store bags.

"I'm good." I tried not to breathe differently as he moved closer. His long hair was pulled back in a ponytail, as it often was when he returned from his violin studio. His *luthier's* studio. That was the official name for a violinmaker, not that he had it on his business cards. Everyone knew what the Fierro family did. "How was your day?" I asked, trying to be a good roomie.

"Fine. Have you eaten anything? Are you hungry?"

"No, I'm good. Blue might be hungry," I said, patting his head.

"I'll feed him." He looked at me a moment. "Have you watched any television? Seen any updates on the news?"

"No. I've been trying to avoid thinking about it."

He rubbed his forehead, then brushed back a lock of escaped hair. "I saw a story about the..." His face looked pained every time he talked about it. "The explosion. The investigators discovered it was a problem with the restaurant downstairs. They'd set up a bypass gas line to the fryer or something, some illegal line that wasn't up to code. The guy responsible..."

His voice trailed off. I knew that the owner of the restaurant had died, along with many of my neighbors. I hadn't known any of them, because I hadn't lived there long enough to forge friendships, but they'd been people, perhaps just waking up and stretching, having morning sex, or brewing a nice cup of coffee. Then bang, gone. The whole tragedy seemed unreal, like a nightmare.

What if I had been there? How would it have felt to die that way? Would I have suffered?

He touched my cheek, drawing me from the darkness. "Don't think about it," he said. "Don't dwell on what might have been."

"It's hard not to."

The touch of his fingertips was gone, leaving too much room for cold. He lifted a couple shopping bags and placed them on the bed beside me. "I picked these up for you today. Nothing fancy."

"You don't have to keep buying me clothes."

"I don't mind."

I took the bags, ashamed that I hadn't gone out myself, or ordered something online by now. "At least let me pay you back."

"Not necessary."

I sat in the window seat to look through the pretty things he'd bought me: more warm sweaters and tops, and an upscale brand of jeans, along with delicate blouses and dark slacks I could wear to work. They were all in my favorite colors, price tags removed. I was already taking up space in his house and eating his food, and now he was buying designer clothes for me. I needed to crawl out of my misery hole and get back to life. "Thank you so much," I said. "You're too generous."

"I just want you to be able to return my mother's clothes." He laughed. "It's jarring to see you wearing them. Do you have money to...you know...get whatever else you need?"

He meant things like bras and underwear. Of course he wouldn't buy me those, in case I misunderstood. "Yes. God, I have money. I'm fine. I can get some things today. I've just been..." I covered my face to hide my blush. "I've been wallowing."

"I get it. I'd wallow too." He glanced at Blue, who'd taken up near-permanent residence in my wallowing bed. "When do you think you might go back to work?"

"The Thursday after New Year's. Met Orchestra management said I could take longer, but I need to get back to it."

"What's on the schedule to play?"

I swallowed hard, trying not to think about my Grapeleaf, exploded in a thousand shards of wood and varnish. Milo's grandmother named all Fierro's violins up until she died a few years ago, and she'd called mine the Grapeleaf because the wood had come from the Mediterranean, and because the tone "flowed like wine." Notable instruments all had names, like children, and were tracked by enthusiasts, as well as the companies that insured them. I'd get money for the loss of my Fierro, but it wouldn't be the same as having it. Somewhere, Fierro registries were being altered with a note next to the Grapeleaf entry. *Lost in an explosion, early 21st century.*

"I think it's Brahms and Mozart." Tears rose in my eyes. Stupid, that I couldn't get over the Grapeleaf. It wasn't like I'd lost a child. "I'll send out some emails to my section mates. Someone will have a violin for me to borrow until..."

Until I found a new instrument, which seemed an impossible task right now, when I couldn't even buy new clothes.

"I have so many violins," Milo said. "Please, take one to use for now. Even the Strad, if you want it."

"Good God. I couldn't."

"You have to play something. Come on. Come take a look at what I have."

I got out of bed to follow him to his instrument room. I'd avoided thinking about the night we'd gone in there, even though the room was just down the hall from my bedroom. I'd pushed down all the memories of him holding me, kissing me, sliding the hard outline of his cock between my legs as he groaned deep in his throat. It was too weird to think about, because he'd been so polite and distant since then.

He ushered me into the room, leaving Blue out in the hall to wait for his dinner. Was it only a week or so ago that he'd showed me his Stradivarius? He opened other cabinets this time, took out a Cecilio and an Amati, a Guarneri, and a Knelling that looked very orange. He had a few Fierros too, and I played each one, but none of them felt like my Grapeleaf. I bowed a few notes on a Pressenda and felt more connection. Milo smiled knowingly. "Similar design, same type of wood as your Fierro," he said. "Although it's a bit older."

I played a few more notes, did a run of scales. It was a great violin. I tried to smile, tried to look happy, but he wasn't fooled.

"Don't worry," he said, his dark eyes holding my gaze. "This is just for now. If you want, we can look for another Fierro together. I have some contacts who might be willing to sell one. Or..." He looked away, then back at me again. "If you want, we can make you a new one. I mean, I can make you one from scratch. It won't be my father's work, like the Grapeleaf, but I can tailor it to you, to your exact specifications."

I felt like the wind had been knocked out of me. People waited years for a violin from Milo's workshop, now that he'd made a name for himself. "Are you serious?"

"I'm very serious, Alice. I'd love to do it. I'd love the challenge of making the perfect instrument for you."

Love to do it. Love to. I love you, even if we're just friends. That's what he was saying. The generosity of his offer brought tears to my eyes.

"Don't cry," he said. "Seriously." He waved a hand through the air. "This room is also dampness-controlled."

I laughed then, instead. "Yes, please. I'd love you to make me one." What could be more special than a violin he made me with his own hands? I'd treasure it beyond bearing. It would be, truly, my own heart, made by the man I loved. "You're going to make me one? Really?"

"Yes. It'll take a while, but if you don't mind waiting a few months..." He touched the Pressenda. "You can play this in the meantime."

I felt like I might choke on my emotions. My heart felt so full. "I don't know what to say. I want to hug you. Can I hug you?"

He gave one of his reticent, reluctant smiles, the ones that made him even more handsome. I put down the Pressenda and threw my arms around him, and there was a little bit of tension between us, but also love. I loved him, even if he wouldn't accept romantic love from me. I adored him. It was okay if he held himself a little stiff, a bit away from me.

He went to the kitchen and fed Blue, then put together a veggie and steak stir-fry for his dinner. All that perfection, and he could cook without breaking a sweat. I wasn't that hungry, so I toasted some tortillas to eat with hummus.

"That smells good," I told him, as we sat at his kitchen counter together.

"I have a secret recipe for the spices."

"Really?"

"No." He laughed. "It comes out of a jar. Want to try a bite?"

"Yes, I freaking do."

He fed me some steak and broccoli, and a slice of green pepper, dangling them from his chopsticks so I could take them into my mouth.

"It's so good, Milo." I might have lost everything, but maybe it was worth it, to have these moments with him. I hadn't even put the claim together for the insurance. I was too damn comfortable here, which was dangerous.

He took a few more bites of his food, swirling the vegetables and steak together in the sauce, then paused and looked over at me. "Do you have any plans for New Year's?"

The tortillas I'd eaten flopped around in my stomach. *Don't get excited, Alice. He doesn't mean it in your fantasy way.* "Uh, no. Not really. I was going to stay in. Stay here, if that's okay."

"That's fine." He pushed his food around and took a breath. "But if you want, you can hang out with me and my friends."

"The paired-up ones? With the girlfriends who only tolerate you?"

"Yeah. If you came with me, you could run interference. Keep the girlfriends occupied while I hang out with my buds."

I burst into laughter, and he smiled. Oh, that smile.

"I'm kidding," he said. "They're great. Juliet and Ella. They've been asking to meet you, so maybe we could all hang out, drink champagne and eat canapés until the ball drops, that kind of thing."

He wore a guarded expression, like he didn't want me to take this the wrong way. I wasn't going to. I was glad to be invited, and curious to meet his friends.

"Thanks for the invite," I said, stealing a bit of steak from his plate and passing it under the counter to Blue. "I'd love to go."

CHAPTER FIVE:
MILO

I had no idea why I'd invited her to New Year's at Fort's house. I wasn't known for being a masochist, but the evening had been booked and planned. My two best friends and their partners were expecting us in half an hour.

"You don't have to dress up," I said, knocking on the guest room door. "They're not fancy."

Well, they were kind of fancy. Fort's father owned the Sinclair Jewelry company, and Devin's family were part owners of Gibraltar Airlines, but my friends themselves were down to earth, for the most part. Fort and Devin were also Dominants, and members of The Gallery. In the past, I'd participated in group scenes with Ella and Juliet, with varying success.

But God, I didn't want Alice to know any of this.

I could trust my friends to be discreet. They knew Alice and I were old friends, and that she was staying with me because of the Michelin building explosion.

"I'm not getting fancy," she said, opening the door. "Just trying to do something with my hair."

God help me, she'd put it up in those wraparound braids. Sometimes I went entire days forgetting Alice was from Sweden, because her English was so good, but then she'd do one of her plaited hairstyles, with gold-red braids circling her head like a Nordic fairy crown. There were always wispy hairs flying loose here and there. She'd tug at them impatiently, while I pondered what was wrong with me that I literally wanted to fuck someone's hairstyle.

"You look nice," I told her. *And I want to fuck your hair, damn you.*

I'd hoped that living with her would take the edge off my lust, but it hadn't, not even a little. She was dressed in one of the outfits I'd bought her. Even though she'd finally gone out shopping for some things, she chose to wear the pink cashmere sweater and dark-washed jeans I'd picked out. With the braided updo and pale pink top, she looked charming and innocent. Good.

No, bad. She still looked fuckable as hell to my traitorous body.

"Let's get out of here," I said.

"I'll get the champagne."

She scooped up the four bottles on the kitchen counter, hugging them to her chest. I laughed and took two of them, ignoring the perky silhouette of her breasts under her sweater. She paused on the way to the door to put on her shoes and say goodbye to Blue.

"Get a coat," I reminded her. "It's cold out." *And I don't want anyone on the street slavering over your breasts. Only me.*

When we arrived at Fort's Blackwell penthouse, a cozy party was already in session. Fort and Juliet welcomed us in, while Devin and Ella waved from the couch.

"You must be Alice," said Juliet, relieving her of the champagne bottles. "Thanks for the booze, and Happy New Year."

"Milo bought the booze, but you're welcome. Thanks for having me over."

"No problem. Any friend of Milo's is a friend of ours. I love your hair!"

Alice patted her glorious crown of braids, looking for wisps, probably, not realizing how beautiful she was. I could tell she was a little overwhelmed. Fort and Juliet's apartment was a showplace, with high ceilings and wall-to-wall windows looking down on the city. The penthouse view made it the perfect place to ring in the New Year. I glanced around at the silver and gold decorations, posters, fringe, and glitter balls, while Alice accepted a "Happy New Year" tiara embellished with lights.

"That looks good on you," I teased. A crown to go on her crown. By the time the intros were finished, Devin and Fort were giving me looks, as if to say, *this is your old family friend? You've fucked her though, right? Or you're planning to?* We could communicate all this through eye contact alone; that was how long we'd trolled for women together—submissive women—before they settled into their current relationships and fell in love.

I ignored their curious glances, settling back in a recliner and digging into the chips. Alice sat at the end of the couch, filling the room Devin and Ella made for her, while Juliet and Fort took the love seat. Conversation flowed easily, as a year-in-retrospective special played on TV in the background.

"Alice," asked Ella, "how long have you and Milo been friends?"

She met my eyes a moment. "Gosh. Forever. My grandfather was a pretty well-known musician in Sweden, and he hit it off with Milo's grandfather while he was buying a Fierro violin. When our fathers both attended the European Conservatory, the families got together often enough to form a bond. We didn't grow up together or anything, but I saw Milo at least a few times every year. Until..."

I picked up the story. "Until I started taking lessons from her father. That was when he worked and taught in Brooklyn. We saw each other a lot then. We were what? How old?"

"I don't remember." She scrunched up her nose. "Were you sixteen? Fifteen? And I was six years younger than you."

"You were the prodigy."

"You keep saying that, Milo, but you were pretty good."

I snorted. "Your father didn't think so."

It felt strange to hash back over our friendship in front of people. The other two couples watched us with bemused looks.

"Anyway," said Alice, "I saw him a lot until my family moved back to Sweden. Then it was only once or twice a year, maybe summer or Christmastime."

"Until now," Devin said.

"Now she sees me all the time," I joked, a nervous reaction to their scrutiny.

"I was so sorry to hear that you lost everything in the Michelin fire," Fort said. "I'm glad Milo was able to offer you a place to stay."

I stared at Alice, unsettled as always when I thought how close I'd come to losing her. "Blue was the one who insisted she stay," I said. "He's taken a shine to her. I doubt he'll ever let her move out now."

Alice laughed, looking around at the others, and the conversation moved to brighter topics. I tried to be bright too, because this was a celebration of a new year and new beginnings, but I soon felt the pull of moodiness. My friends and their girlfriends were so happy together, so at ease, because they'd been aware of each other's kinks from the start. Fort and Juliet met outside a BDSM club, and Devin and Ella had participated in a dungeon scene together before they'd even met.

I studied Alice, the way she moved, the way she talked. Was there something submissive in the way she lowered her eyes, or positioned her body? Any clues in the way she sat or moved her hands? It was a stretch. I usually sensed these things in submissives I met, and I didn't sense them in Alice, but maybe that was because I'd known her for so long.

Did she sense she was in a room of profoundly kinky people? Most likely not.

Juliet poured another round of champagne as midnight crept closer. I wasn't drunk enough, but I didn't dare drink more. One look from Alice, one innocent kiss at midnight could easily go sideways if I let down my guard.

When the conversation came back around to music, and Alice's job with the New York Metropolitan Orchestra, she told my friends I was making her a new violin to replace her other one. Once again, Fort and Dev threw me speculative looks. Juliet clasped her hands to her heart.

"That's so romantic."

They all laughed, and I forced a smile. "I'm not known for my romantic gestures, but I'm happy to do it. I rarely get to make instruments for friends, especially friends with the talent to appreciate my efforts."

Alice's eyes shone as she met my gaze. "I'm still so excited that you offered. I can't explain how much it means to me."

She meant those words for my friends, but I was the one who couldn't look away. To my left, Devin and Ella put their heads together, whispering. They were both pretty drunk. Fort and Juliet, as hosts, weren't drunk, just buzzed. I downed an entire glass of champagne, and Juliet refilled it for me with a secret smile. Like my parents, my friends wanted me to settle down with someone nice.

Like my parents, they didn't understand how difficult it was for me when it came to my feelings for Alice, the back and forth of caring for her at the same time I wanted to destroy her in bed. I could see Devin and Ella start kissing in my peripheral vision. They'd been drawn to each other from the beginning, even though Ella had held him off for a while in self-preservation. I doubted they'd even notice when the ball dropped at midnight.

There's nothing worse than spending New Year's Eve with happy couples. I remembered Alice saying that in my car, the night of my parents' party. On the other side of me, Fort stared at Juliet, then away, like his love for her was too much to deal with.

"I think I'll go out on your balcony for some air," I said, getting to my feet.

"It's almost midnight," said Fort.

"I'll come back before then."

Mean of me, to leave Alice in there with them when she barely knew them, but if I didn't get away from all their lovey-dovey moon eyes, I was going to lose my mind. I walked through the kitchen to Fort's spacious covered patio, his porch in the sky. In the summer, walls of vines provided shade, but in the winter, the vines died back and let in the wind. I hugged myself, looking out at the skyline. Should have brought a coat. Shouldn't have come in the first place. Alice was right, happy couples were the worst.

You could be in a happy couple if you wanted, my subconscious whispered. It was true. There were plenty of hardcore maso subs at The Gallery who would be interested in a relationship with me. They were fun women, all of them, and easy to get along with. Many times, I'd considered asking one of them out, but the deeper connection wasn't there. What was this curse, that a girl I'd called Lala for half my life would end up growing into the woman my soul pined for?

"Milo?"

Her voice drew me from my thoughts, and I turned before I gentled my frown. She looked apologetic. "I just thought you might like your coat," she said, bringing it to me.

"Thank you." I managed a smile, noting her own coat, wrapped hastily around her shoulders. "Want to join me? There's a great view."

She took up a place beside me, and we scanned the surrounding buildings together, finding the lit-up area of Times Square. "Have you ever gone to Times Square on New Year's Eve?" she asked.

"Hell no. It's too cold, with too many crowds."

"I used to see the feeds on TV in Sweden. I always wondered if you were there, since you were my only friend in Manhattan." She grinned. "I had this idea that I might catch a glimpse of you."

"There are a lot of people there. Hard to pick out any one person." I looked over at her profile, and those damn braids. "You should put your coat on and button it up. I think it's getting colder." I couldn't resist helping her, touching her soft fleece coat, brushing my fingertips over one shoulder as I straightened the warm garment. "I don't even know why I'm out here. Too much champagne inside," I joked. "I don't want to get wasted."

"Devin and Ella are pretty far gone," she said with a laugh. "But I like your friends. I love the way you're all so comfortable around each other."

"I told you they weren't fancy."

We settled into silence. I wasn't touching her, but I wanted to be. She was close enough to touch, close enough to pull into my arms, but I resisted the urge and shoved my hands in my pockets.

"Here's to a better year," she said softly, turning away from the wind. "This year wasn't all bad, but it could have been better."

"Here's to a better year," I agreed. "We need some champagne to clink on it."

"How about a high five?"

"That works." Awkward, so awkward to exchange high fives. Why didn't I just confess my true feelings, now, with the view and the wind? *Alice, I love you so much that I can't let myself have you. That's how deep you live in my heart.*

Juliet knocked on the glass, getting our attention, and held up five fingers before she disappeared.

"Five minutes until the ball drops," I said. We could hear the rising wave of sound from Times Square. "I guess we should be good guests and go inside."

"Yeah, they'll want us in there for the countdown."

I followed her, gazing down at her beautiful hair, and yes, her gorgeous ass that was perfectly framed by her jeans. By the time we got to the living room, all of them were standing up, champagne glasses in hand. We grabbed ours, and I took a sip for Alice's sake. Yes, to a better year. I'd do everything in my power to make it better for her. The hosts nattered on TV, small talk about New Year's resolutions, as the crowd drunkenly sang *Auld Lang Syne*. Ella and Devin shared champagne between kisses, and Fort and Juliet stood together, grinning, wrapped in each other's arms.

5... 4... 3... 2... 1...

The fireworks on TV were echoed by live fireworks outside the window, booming like bombs. While the couples around us kissed, Alice met my gaze. I took her hand without thinking, and she stood still, waiting. She was waiting for me to kiss her, wasn't she? It made no sense not to kiss her when everyone else was kissing, and I stared at her lips, wanting to taste them. Just a peck. Nothing serious, just a brush of my lips against hers...

Devin nudged me, nodding toward Fort and Juliet. Their heads were bowed together as they gazed down at the engagement ring Fort had put on her finger a couple months earlier. This was the year they'd become husband and wife. They embraced, kissing with all the passion of a couple who'd decided to stay together their entire lives. What a crazy leap of faith. Well, Fort had always been the responsible one, so of course he'd be engaged first. Devin teased Fort about "saying goodbye to the good life," but he'd probably be engaged to Ella by the end of this new year.

As for Alice and me, the opportunity for a New Year's kiss had passed. Instead, we watched the others, and listened to their settled-couple chatter. They were so happy, and I was happy for them, but I felt fucking sad, because happy couples were the worst.

CHAPTER SIX:
ALICE

Blue poked his head in my door, and I beckoned him to join me in my empty, cold bed.

"Sorry we were late getting home tonight," I said, when he'd settled down beside me. "It was New Year's. Do you know what that is? A new beginning?" I stroked his head as he looked at me with his deeply communicative eyes. "You should know. You got a new beginning when Milo adopted you. What was it like to run around that dog track, and live in a noisy, smelly kennel all the time?"

Blue gave a soft sniff and snuggled closer to me.

"That bad? I believe it. I hate running, and a kennel isn't nearly as nice as this place." I laid back and stared up at the ceiling. "What is it about me, Blue? Does he still see me as a kid? As 'Lala'? Does he worry about us competing as violinists? We have completely different styles, and we've chosen different career paths."

Blue stretched his long, thin legs, pointing his toes and yawning. He wanted petting, not questions, and he was ready to fall asleep.

59

"Okay," I said, scratching his ears. "I know it's past your bedtime."

I kept the rest of my thoughts to myself, like the thought that Milo just didn't see me as girlfriend material. I'd never have a heartfelt scene like the one Juliet had experienced tonight, thinking about a wedding with the man she loved most in the world.

Maybe it was my odd coloring, my light green eyes and blonde-ginger hair. Maybe I was too tall, or too focused on my career. Maybe my breasts weren't big enough, or my feet were too big. Ugh. I cuddled around the curve of Blue's body and tried, without success, to fall asleep as peacefully as him.

CHAPTER SEVEN:
MILO

I scanned the tables at Coleman's, looking for Fort's dark hair and Devin's blond crew cut. Our weekly Saturday night dinners had been scaled back to once a month, since my friends rarely attended The Gallery afterward anymore. I was okay with it, because Juliet and Ella made them happy. When I located the table, I noted that they both looked way more relaxed than I did.

"Hi," I said, sliding into a chair. "What are you boys drinking?"

"A Saint-Emilion merlot," said Dev. "Have some. It's a spectacular vintage."

I raised a hand and called to the waiter. "Can I get a scotch?"

My friends exchanged a look as Devin put down the wine bottle. "Things aren't getting any easier, I see."

"Not really."

Alice had been living at my place for almost a month now, leaving her scent, beauty, and energy all over my apartment, her strands of light hair, her coffee cups and charging cables. Before, she'd been a distant fantasy. Now she was always close, and too real. Worse, she believed that I didn't want her, when the truth was that I *couldn't* want her.

"It's fucking frustrating," I said, as our waiter deposited a neat scotch in front of me.

"I can see how it would be," said Fort. "You're living with a woman, while reaping none of the usual benefits."

Devin tsked. "Have some class, man. He's trying to be a good guy." He turned to me. "Any timeline on her new place?"

I shrugged. "Even if she finds a new apartment she likes, which she hasn't, it'll take a while to close on it, and she hasn't had much time to look since she went back to work. I'd offer to help her find something, but I don't want her to feel pressured to leave."

We paused to order our steaks—Coleman's specialty—while I downed another swallow of scotch. After the waiter left, Devin tapped his fingers on the table and gave me one of his lofty, airline-pilot looks.

"I've been thinking about you and your 'family friend' Alice." His light blue eyes fixed on me in the noisy restaurant. "You need to say something to her about your kinky fuckery, you know, slip it into some conversation. At least hint at it."

"*Hint* at it?"

"Yeah, like, give her a Dom look, or play with your belt while she's around. What if she's kinky too? What if she's a Grade A submissive masochist? I mean, if she's attracted to you..."

I'd told them a little about our Strad night makeout session, although I hadn't told them about her wanting to marry me, because they'd never leave that alone.

"I'm not exactly the 'Gallery' Milo when I'm around her," I said.

"It doesn't matter. The 'Gallery' Milo is still there," said Fort. "There's always the undercurrent. That's why kinky radar works, why perverts usually recognize each other."

I pointed at the two of them. "Both of you met your matches in or around BDSM clubs. It had nothing to do with radar."

"All Fort's saying is that she's into you, and you're into her. You have been for a long time. There's got to be something going on there, you know, subliminally. Does she have any submissive-like traits?"

Fort and I both snorted at "submissive-like traits," but I considered Devin's question. She definitely triggered the Dominant in me. It was something about her sweetness, and the light, trusting quality of her character. And the one time I'd kissed her...

I couldn't stop thinking about the way she'd melted against me when I kissed her, like she would have accepted anything I did to her. That was why she scared me, because I imagined she *was* willing to accept whatever I wanted to do, whatever urge I wanted to play out on her yielding body.

Fuck, I was getting hard. I shifted in my chair and drank more scotch, not that alcohol helped.

"It's possible she has some submissive tendencies," I admitted. "It's actually probable, but I don't know if she's into pain, which is my main fetish. I don't know if she's a masochist."

"Come on, Milo," Dev scoffed. "She's a classical violinist."

"Joking aside," said Fort, as I frowned at Devin, "we don't know that she's *not* a masochist. If you came out to her with the BDSM side of yourself, and she was amenable, you could start playing around with power exchange scenes and see how far things developed."

"But where would they end?" I asked. "Where do our power exchange hookups always end? At The Gallery, with consensual non-consent, heavy pain, and sharing partners, and I don't..."

Fort and Devin exchanged another amused look. "You don't want to do that to her," Fort said, finishing my sentence. "Hmm, where have I heard that before? Maybe from every Dom at The Gallery who's started a serious relationship? The ones who love each other find a way to make it work."

"You don't understand. I really can't do those things to her."

"Why not?"

They both looked at me, eyebrows raised. I drained the last of my scotch and banged it on the table. "Because she's Lilly-Alice Nyquist, and she trusts me, and she thinks I'm this amazing guy."

"You are pretty amazing," Dev said, batting his eyes at me.

"It's your angsty long hair, and your eyes, and the way you make those instruments," Fort agreed, playing along.

"Fuck you both."

"Here's the thing," said Dev. "You keep saying she's this untouchable family friend, but I'm pretty sure she wants you to touch her. Like, *really* touch her."

"I wish I could." I let out a frustrated sigh. "It's partly the family thing, the friendship dynamic. I've known this girl my whole life. My parents dragged me to her fucking christening when I was in first grade. Her christening, you know, crying infant, baptismal font, long white dress?"

"We're degenerates, but we know what christenings are, Massimiliano," Dev drawled.

Fort's hazel eyes widened at a sudden, perverse thought. "How many of us get a chance to work over a sub we met at her *christening?* I don't understand how you're not all over this opportunity, man."

I called for another scotch, and they changed the subject to ward off my rising temper. They talked about work instead, and their blissfully well-adjusted relationships, which only made me feel worse. We made it through the salad and main course before they started again on my fucked-up situation with my painfully tempting roommate.

"You know, Milo, you could conceivably start a relationship with Alice and *not* take her to The Gallery," said Fort. "You could keep things mildly kinky at home, show her as much of your dark side as you felt comfortable with, and visit the club when you needed to let loose. Lots of Gallery people play outside their traditional relationships. As long as both partners are okay with it, no one gets hurt. Well, except in ways they like to get hurt."

"Yeah, I considered something like that for about ten seconds. Here's the shit thing." I scowled, pushing my plate away. "I don't want to play at The Gallery with someone else. I want to connect that way with her, and it's so fucking wrong."

"Why?" Dev frowned at me. "Who says it's wrong? It's an expression of your sexuality, and she may be on board with it. You don't know, because you're too chickenshit to explore the possibilities."

"There are no possibilities."

"For all you know, she's a raging maso subslut who's just waiting for you to reach out and choke her and cane her, and fuck her up the ass."

"No." My loud, sharp denial rung out in the restaurant, and Fort held up a hand, silencing both of us until the people at the other tables turned back to their food. "No," I repeated more quietly, staring at Devin. "Even if she begged me for that, I couldn't do it to her. That's what you don't understand."

"That's such a Dominant thing," Devin said. "*If I love her, why do I want to hurt her?*"

"Hey, Dev," said Fort, the peacemaker. "Maybe you should let it drop."

My lips flattened and my hands made fists beside the table as I imagined hurting Alice, binding her, fucking her mouth and her ass, forcing her to service me. I wanted it, and I hated myself for wanting it.

Then I thought about sharing her per The Gallery's rules, letting someone else do those things to her, and my mind shut down. "No," I said for the third time, shaking my head. "Just no."

"So you're basically fucked," said Devin, after an appropriate silence. "It's going to be hard for you, living with her, pushing all that stuff down. Hey, I wonder if Ella's apartment is still open, the one her science foundation provided before she moved in with me?"

"Hmm," I said.

"Want me to ask her about it? It's not that far from where Alice works."

"It's probably not available anymore."

"I'll text Ella."

I put a hand over his before he could get out his phone. "No. Like I said, I don't want her to feel pressured to leave. Anyway, she's still processing what happened, so I think it's better for her to be around someone who can look after her. It was a hard loss. Especially the violin. Let me get this," I said, as the waiter brought the bill.

Neither one tried to stop me. I owed them, for acting like a jackass. We had our codes.

"It's nice of you to make her a new Fierro," Devin said. "Have you started it?"

"I've got the wood." It was a relief to talk about something besides hurting Alice. "This violin has to be perfect, you know? I got all the wood pieces from Eastern Europe, which has the best quality and density. I've got a contact I trust."

"She's lucky," said Fort. "I think she's going to get a really special instrument."

"I hope so. Anyway, thanks for meeting up tonight. I needed it. Sorry I behaved like a prick."

"You're always a prick with the scotch," joked Devin. "No worries."

"No, seriously, I'll find my way through this. I don't want to lose my closest friends in the process."

"We've been through shit before," said Fort. "Everything will turn out okay."

I nodded, wishing I shared his positive outlook. Dev gave me a nudge. "So, not sure if this is a good time to ask, but are you going to The Gallery tonight?"

"Not sure. You guys?"

I knew even before they made their excuses that they probably weren't going to go. In a weird way, I felt like I shouldn't go because of

Alice, even though she'd be at work for another hour, playing with the orchestra. Maybe she'd want to go to a movie afterward, something to take her mind off things. Maybe I could catch the end of her performance.

Maybe I should go to The Gallery to take care of my urges so I'm not fantasizing about her every time she walks by me.

"I might go," I said. "I should go there and play hard with someone, and really work things out."

"Lucky woman," laughed Fort. "I can think of a few regulars who'd volunteer for the privilege of slaking your violent lusts."

Violent, vile, dangerous lusts. After I said goodbye to them, I walked home and took the elevator straight up to The Gallery's floor. It was busy in the multi-level dungeon. There were indeed several subs I had experience playing with, and their eyes followed me as I skulked around the club's perimeter. *I could tie Catherine up there. I could fuck Sarah there. I could use that whip on Bailey and make her scream.*

But I wasn't in the mood, and there were too many people around when I didn't feel like being social. I ended up leaving twenty minutes after I arrived, wondering if my sex life was over forever, or just until Alice moved out of my place.

CHAPTER EIGHT: ALICE

I walked along 19th Street, watching for the Fierro Violins storefront. I'd been there before—I knew exactly what block it was on—but it always seemed like a surprise to stumble across it, because it was hidden among much larger businesses.

Not that Fierro Violins was a small place. When I walked into the lobby, I took in the familiar high walls, the stone fireplace, and the deep, heavy club chairs that welcomed clients to sit. I knew there was a warren of workshops in the back, and dozens of artisans who worked for the family.

"Good morning. Can I help you?"

The polite receptionist stood and approached me, at the same time Milo appeared in the doorway at the back. His eyes met mine, and I was struck, as always, by how handsome he was, even in a worn, stained, leather apron.

"You made it," he said as I crossed to him. God, that smile.

I ducked under his arm as he held the door for me. "I said I would come."

"You were fast asleep when I left. Snoring."

I rolled my eyes. "Musicians sleep in on Mondays. Well, except for you." We walked down the hall, which was quieter than you'd expect a music-based workplace to be. I mentioned this to Milo and he raised his brows.

"You don't make a violin with hammers and power tools. What you hear is the silence of concentration."

I gave him a look, and he smiled again. It felt like a personal victory whenever he smiled at me, because he wasn't the smiley type. He led me down the corridor to the last workshop on the left, a wood-paneled cocoon of violin parts and instruments in process. The still, cool air smelled like varnish and cut wood. There were so many tools, so many pieces and molds, and raw slabs of wood.

He took one of them in his hand and turned to me. "This is going to be the back of your violin. It's the only piece I have so far, but it's perfect."

I took the oblong piece of wood. It was heavier than I thought, and sanded smooth. I held it to my cheek. "It's magnificent, Milo."

"It's from an old-growth maple on the north side of a mountain in the Caucasus. It was cut decades ago, but it's been drying. I think it's just right."

I rubbed my cheek against the dull-colored slab from halfway across the world, and thought how random it was, that this tree had been planted maybe two hundred years ago, and now it had come to me, to make beautiful music. It would be cut and shaped and varnished a rich auburn color. "Is it drier wood than my last violin?" I asked.

Milo shrugged. "Probably about the same. We don't use crap wood at Fierro." But his eyes were bright. He was excited. It was probably a really special cut of wood. I wondered how much he'd paid for it. He'd never give me a straight answer, so I didn't bother to ask.

"Thank you," I said instead. "I really can't thank you enough for doing this."

He took the wood back, placed it on one of the workshop's nearest counters, and walked to another counter to pick up a completed violin. "I wanted you to play for me while you were here. This is a prototype, for taking measurements, so I can really nail the specifications."

"Oh. Sure." I tipped the violin onto my shoulder, nestling it beneath my chin. "What should I play?"

"Nothing yet." He drew out a battered measuring tape and measured the space between my chin and the end of the instrument, as well as the chin rest. He measured the length of my forearm, and waited patiently for me to compose myself when I giggled and ducked away. "It tickles. I'm sorry."

"No worries."

He took a few more measurements, and then I started playing some Vivaldi. He didn't film me, or take photos, but I'd never been so closely scrutinized in my life. His dark eyes seemed to blaze at me from a couple feet away. I tried to play normally, without any reservations, and I was careful not to turn my head, even when he circled me with that intense stare.

"You're going to make such a tone on this new violin," he said, when I finished a short gavotte. "Play something slower now."

It was an order, delivered in his rough, sexy voice. My fingers shook as perverse thoughts filled my brain, to the point where it was hard to concentrate. I could smell him, feel him beside me. He was checking out my angles while I refocused on musicality, because, by God, I wanted to impress him. I played one of my favorite meditative songs, Barber's *Adagio for Strings*. After a while, I knew Milo wasn't collecting specs anymore; he was listening.

I flicked a glance over at him, catching his gaze. "Is that enough?" I asked. "Or do you want me to keep going?"

"Keep going."

I ended the Barber and began an allegro piece, one Milo used to play during lessons with my father. I wondered if he'd remember, but then he smiled, and I played faster because I was flirting. Milo was a temptation I couldn't shake. He'd made it clear we were going to keep things friendly, especially while I was living at his apartment, but that only made me want him more.

I looked at the wall beyond his shoulder as I plied the strings, but I could still feel his eyes on me. I could feel them tracing over the lines of my jaw, and the lines of the violin as my bow arced between us. Then he picked up a violin from the rack above his work counter, as well as a bow. He joined the piece mid-phrase, angling his body so our violins sang together.

Without thought, we played off each other, blending the small tone differences in our instruments the way experienced musicians did, communicating with our aural senses, rather than sight or words. I closed my eyes, feeling the notes dance between us. Sweeping glissandos, trembling vibrato battling for the most perfect resonance. I wanted to play slower so the song would never end, but I had to keep up with him, to make the perfection last. When we played the last notes, I opened my eyes and found him staring at me.

There was hot desire in his gaze. I wasn't imagining it. It would be such a little thing, to put down the instruments and reach out to one another. Why didn't he want it? Why didn't I force the issue?

"That was awesome." I put the violin in my lap, my mouth half open, wanting to say the rest of the words. *I want you. I love you. Please touch me.*

"We make good music together," he said, before I could come up with anything. His words were brisk as he turned away.

"Yes, we do." I wanted him to turn back and face me. I wanted to fight with him over this shit. I had all this energy to give him, but he was behind a wall and I couldn't reach him, and it made me want to smash something. I looked down at the violin, and forced my fingers to unwind from the neck. "You'd better take this back."

"Sure." He turned to me, meeting my eyes for one burning moment. "If I need to know anything else about how you play, I know where to find you."

"I guess you do."

"I may be home late tonight."

He moved away again. Always moving away from me.

"It's your life," I said. "I'll see you when I see you."

I left Fierro Violins, feeling wrought up with emotion. In the last hour, I'd been excited, hopeful, grateful, in love, miserable, and furious. I had the afternoon and evening off—all the time in the world to wallow in my feelings. I walked in the cold all the way to the Bridgeport building, stopping to get food for my lonely dinner, then went upstairs.

"You like me, at least," I said, as Blue trotted over to welcome me. "Yes, I missed you, sweetie. Milo won't be home for dinner, so it's just you and me. Feel like a shower?"

Blue didn't like showers, but I needed one. I was freezing, plus I didn't want the smell of wood and violins on me, and the memory of our impromptu duet, the way our tones had blended so wonderfully together. I took my time, standing under the steamy water, trying to clear my mind. While Blue hovered, I put on pajamas and a robe and sat in front of my laptop, logging on to a website for Manhattan real estate. So many choices. So expensive. So many tasks to follow up on.

I needed to find a place to stay, so I could remove myself from the situation, but the insurance morass, in my current mood, seemed an insurmountable task to untangle. I closed my laptop and drifted out to the kitchen, and decided I didn't want to cook. A salad and a handful of cookies would be fine. Forget the salad. Just cookies.

I took my extremely unhealthy dinner into Milo's living room and flopped on his couch. Blue curled up beside the ornate fireplace, drawing in his tail and legs until he was a perfect oval. I ate a couple cookies with milk, then took the rest back to the kitchen, because they were only making me feel worse.

I left the kitchen and walked down the hall, and stood in the door of Milo's master bedroom. He kept the door open while he was away, and Blue went in and out, but I hadn't felt bold enough yet to do the same. I wished I had the nerve to sneak in and poke through his closets and drawers, or do what I really wanted, which was to sprawl face down in the middle of his bed and bury my face in his covers. I wanted so badly to watch him while he slept, but he kept the door shut when he was in there.

Jesus, Alice, you need to get a life, or at least your own place.

I backed away from his open bedroom door and went back down the hall, past my room and Milo's office, to the instrument room, another place I didn't dare trespass. I was afraid Milo's priceless-instrument room had a hidden security camera. At the very least, I might mess up the climate-controlled air by breathing too hard or drooling. I walked past with Blue at my heels, and glanced at the next door. Then I stopped.

What was in there? It was probably the closet with all the climate-control equipment. Was there a secret camera set up, or no? Milo's whole ritzy, glitzy apartment fascinated me. I put my hand on the knob, driven by curiosity. The door wasn't locked. I looked down at Blue, whose dark eyes gave away nothing. "If I open this, will I set off an alarm?" I asked.

When Blue didn't answer, I turned the knob the rest of the way and pushed the door open. Light from the hallway illuminated the darkness, stretching to a far back wall. It wasn't a closet after all, and it didn't contain any climate-control machinery. There was no security camera. In fact, it seemed to be another complete room, deeper than the instrument room. I fumbled beside the doorjamb for a light.

"Coming in?" I asked Blue over my shoulder.

He made a small, snuffling sound and trotted away. I finally found a panel of light switches and flicked one on. Fixtures around the baseboards came on, casting up dim, white light in the larger-than-expected space. At first I only saw shapes and shadows. I took a couple more steps inside, realizing the room was L-shaped. There were cabinets along the outside wall, and a bed tucked away in the back. Was this another guest room?

Was that even a bed?

I walked toward it. The white-sheeted mattress had a lattice of bars for a headboard, and tall posts at either end of the footboard, with rings attached to the posts at the middle and top. I wasn't sure how long it took me to realize it wasn't a bed for sleeping on. Maybe a couple seconds, maybe a couple minutes of frantic thought while I stood there wringing my hands. It was a sex bed. A bondage bed.

As I processed that, the dark shapes around me took on more recognizable forms.

A bondage chair. A padded bench with adjustable features. Three different types of racks: an X-shaped one, a rectangular one, and an arch, all of them with attachment points like the ones on the bed posts. I was in a BDSM dungeon. Milo's dungeon.

I went back to the light panel and lit up everything in the room. There were randomly placed lamps, overhead lights, and a wrought iron chandelier over the bondage bed. I couldn't believe what I was looking at, but also, I couldn't believe I hadn't figured this out before.

Milo was kinky. By the looks of things, he was extremely kinky. This was what had been holding him back from me sexually, what he'd been trying to protect me from. This was why he'd done nothing more than kiss me, when I obviously wanted to go further.

Milo, you idiot. I don't care. In fact, I think I love you more.

Like the rest of his place, his sexy dungeon was fantastic, elegant, old-world, rich. With the lights on, I could see the sheen of polish on the wood structures, and the dark metal's smooth, heavy quality. What did he do in here? My imagination ran wild, along with my jealousy. How many women had he brought in here? Not me. He never would have shown this to me if I hadn't stumbled into it on my own.

When would he be home? I didn't want him to catch me in here, perving his collection of kinkiness, but I couldn't stop looking at everything. I opened the cabinets and closed them again without touching anything, overwhelmed by the things I saw inside. Sex toys and dildos.

Butt plugs. Nipple clamps. Bondage equipment. Chains, rope, gags, and leather whips and straps, designed to cause pain.

Oh God, what if there was a camera in here? What if there was a silent alarm that was already beckoning him home, so he could accost whoever had broken into his secret sex lair? What would he say if he caught me here? I knew a little about BDSM, but I'd never done anything kinky with a partner. I knew there were Dominants and submissives in this lifestyle, and it was clear to me which one he was, based on the way he'd kissed me that one time.

How could I have been so clueless, so blind to these proclivities in him? It seemed so obvious now. His deep, brusque voice and his intent eye contact, his commanding manner... All my life, I'd known he was a dark kind of guy. So much was explained by this dungeon, but so many more questions were raised. How long had it taken him to amass this collection of furniture and toys? How many partners had he played with? How many did he have right now? Was I in the way, since I'd moved in here? Was he seeing some other woman right now, some secret slave he couldn't invite over until I moved out again?

I rubbed my forehead, wondering what to do. Walk out of this room and shut the door? Pretend I didn't know this dungeon was here, just a few doors down from my room? Why didn't he keep a room like this locked?

Because he'd lived alone until now. *You're trespassing. You're invading his privacy.*

It was crazy, how you could know someone for so long, but not really know them at all. I'd only seen what I wanted to see, the moody, mostly solitary violinist who was a few years older than me, old enough to seem wise beyond his years. Now I was picturing him in here, looking in the cabinets for the perfect cuffs, the blindfold, the rope to fix a woman—me—to one of these benches or racks. It was a Milo I'd never thought about, but one that made me shiver with desire. Bound, blindfolded, at his mercy...

What would he do then? Whip me? Fuck me? Call me a naughty slut?

Was all of this—the dungeon, the perversity—the reason he kept me at arm's length? *I can't do this, because I respect you too much.* I remembered his words because they'd disappointed me so deeply.

But now...

Now everything could be different. I could let him know I was okay with this side of him. In fact, as I stood looking around at the forbidding furniture and tall cabinets, I knew this side of him was a huge part of what attracted me. Milo was good at so many things. He was kind and caring, and renowned for making instruments. He was a noted musician, who played the violin with the potency of someone who needed to do it to live. If he was good at this BDSM stuff too...

Oh God. I had to process all this, and I had to get out of here before he caught me lurking. I made sure everything was just as it had been when I entered, turned out the lights, and scurried out the door, shutting it behind me. Blue came trotting back, ready to be fawned over again. I complied, petting his smooth head and scratching him behind the ears.

"Why didn't you tell me?" I asked. "Why didn't you explain things to me?"

He let out a snuffle, like I was ridiculous. I probably was. I should have figured this out sooner, but it wasn't too late to make things work between us. I went back to my room and started an Internet search on BDSM, because by the looks of things, the information I'd picked up in books and movies wouldn't be enough.

CHAPTER NINE:
MILO

I arrived home after midnight, wanting to lose myself in sleep, but I couldn't sleep. After work, after Alice had visited my workshop, I'd gone to a friend's house, to her "birthday bash," which was more of a birthday gangbang. Allie was into that stuff, and it was fun seeing her get all her masochistic buttons pushed, but I wasn't in the mood to participate. Instead of Allie, I kept thinking of Alice. Their names were similar—only one letter difference—but the two of them were nothing alike.

Alice was sweet and low-key, while Allie was a tempest. Alice had light hair, and Allie was dark. Alice was tall, and Allie was a petite package of perversity. I'd done so many fun scenes with Allie over the years, and now...now I couldn't get into her. At all.

Fuck. Alice was ruining my life, tearing me in two, forcing me to be someone respectable because she was respectable. The other Doms were back at Allie's, having a fucking blast, and I was lying in bed, too disgusted with myself to even jack off. I wanted what the guys at Allie's place wanted, to torment and fuck a pretty girl, but I wanted it to be Alice instead, and that was a fucking problem.

I rolled over with a groan, squeezing my eyes shut. It didn't help. I pictured everything I wanted to do to Lilly-Alice Nyquist in pornographic detail. There was the hard blowjob, of course. Fantasy number one: ramming my cock into her throat as she struggled to stay on her knees. I'd keep one hand clenched in her hair, making her look up at me every so often so I could see the tears overflowing her eyes. Her gagging and sputtering would be music to my ears—

No. Fucking no. Don't think about her like that.

I had more, much more where that came from. There was the fantasy of cuffing her hands over her head and whipping her with a crop or strap as she struggled to get away, pleading with me to show her mercy. Maybe her hair would be done up in those braids, and I'd unravel them when I stopped to let her draw a breath. I'd shove her head back and kiss her hard, and clasp my fingers around her slender neck until she made frantic, panicked sounds.

No, don't jack off to that, you sick pervert. Not to choking out Lilly-Alice.

Fine. I'd jack off to the anal fantasies instead. I'd imagine her long legs held apart by a spreader, her ass in the air, bent over a trestle or bench. I'd toy with her first, humiliate her, insert a plug that made her squirm, all the while reminding her that my dick was bigger and harder than the plug, than anything she'd fucking imagined. When I started easing into her, her toes would curl, and her asshole would clench in alarm. I'd spank her and whisper threats in her ear. *Let me in. I'm going to make you my anal-craving slut.*

I almost didn't hear the tap at the door over the roar of blood filling my cock. The object of my fantasies opened the door and stuck her head in. Shit, those braids again. I could see them in the dim light from the hall.

"Milo? Are you awake?"

I should have played dead, but I'd already turned toward the door to see if she was okay.

"I'm awake. What's wrong?"

"Nothing's wrong." That was what she said, but there was clearly something troubling her. "Can I come in?" she asked.

"Sure."

I sat up, wishing I slept in more than boxers as I clicked on my bedside light. Fortunately, my massive erection had ebbed, but I still piled as many covers as I could in my lap. She'd picked the wrong time to come visiting. I watched, holding my breath, as she came into my bedroom and stood at the bottom of my bed.

"I'm sorry, Milo. I know it's late. I should probably just wait, or maybe not say anything, but if I don't say something now, I'll never find the courage again."

I braced as she covered her eyes. What was she going to tell me? What dramatic, heartfelt revelation was going to make me want her even more?

"You can talk to me about anything," I said.

She eyed my bare chest, and I wondered if she could see my heart beating. She was in a sleeveless white cotton nightgown. Nothing frilly, just practical. So Nordic. Kind of virginal.

"Tell me what's on your mind," I said, before I could start having dirty thoughts about it.

She met my gaze, her eyes wide, her features pale and lovely. "Milo, I accidentally... Well, I sort of stumbled on... I went into your...dungeon...today."

The breath I'd been holding hardened to an ache in my chest. I let it out, wishing she'd said anything else, any other thing in the world besides *I went into your dungeon today.*

"Milo...?" she said in a soft voice.

I didn't say anything at first, couldn't say anything, but I felt anger and a dark sense of betrayal. I kept the dungeon's door closed for a reason. I ought to have installed a lock when she moved in, but that would only have drawn attention to it. "I wish you hadn't found that," I finally said.

"I'm sorry. I was wandering around with Blue. I felt restless. I love your apartment so I was looking at the rooms and then I saw that door, and I thought it was a closet, something to do with the music room, so I went in, and once I was in there, I couldn't stop myself from looking at all the...equipment."

"You were creeping around my apartment?" I asked. "Opening all my doors?"

"It wasn't locked."

"That doesn't mean you're welcome to go in."

She stood, facing me with her arms crossed over her chest. "I'm sorry if I intruded on your privacy, but you shouldn't feel embarrassed."

"Shouldn't I? Would you be embarrassed if you were in my position? If I'd wanted you to know about that...that room...I would have told you."

"I wish you had told me." She stuck out her chin, her eyes alight with flaring anger. "I wish I had known. It would have explained a lot of things about you."

I was surprised she had the audacity to scold me for my secrecy, considering she was the one who'd done something so wrong. I was angry and embarrassed, even more so than her. I wanted to order her out of my room, wanted to yell at her, *You shouldn't be in here, especially to tell me this.*

"I could have pretended I never found it," she said in the fraught silence. "But we're closer friends than that. I wanted you to know that I saw it, and that I know now that you're into BDSM, but I don't care. It doesn't scare me. It actually..." Her blush deepened. "It makes me curious."

I had to laugh at that. Curious? She had no fucking idea.

"Why are you laughing?" She tossed her head, with her beautiful intricate braids. "Why aren't you saying anything?"

"Because it's none of your business. If I wanted you to know about that side of me, I would have told you. I would have said, *hey, Alice, I'm into BDSM. Want to check out my dungeon?*"

"Why didn't you want me to know?"

"Because it's private."

"Is this why you won't consider a relationship with me? Because you think I won't accept this side of you? You're wrong about that. I'm not afraid of passion...and...and sexy stuff."

I laughed again. "*Sexy stuff?*"

"Whatever. Whatever craziness you're into, it doesn't scare me."

"I'm not sure you have enough information to say that."

"You think I'm too innocent?"

"I know you're too innocent." Why was I even sitting in my bed discussing this with her? Why hadn't I sent her out of my room yet? "Alice, it's really late, and I don't want to talk about this with you."

"Too bad. I want to talk about it with you."

"Obviously. You came in my bedroom while I was half asleep and dropped this on me, but I don't want to discuss it."

"I'm not that innocent," she insisted, standing her ground in her ridiculously innocent white nightie. If she knew how much I wanted to tear it off her...

"Alice." I rubbed my eyes. "Go to bed. This is a part of myself that I want to keep separate from you. Please respect that."

"I don't want to," she said, her voice trembling. "I'm trying to tell you that I'm into what you're into. I mean, I could be into it. I'm really interested in BDSM and power exchange, and I think it would be awesome to play with you. You know, do a 'scene.'"

She was throwing out vocabulary, trying to sound like she knew what she was talking about. Poor, misguided girl.

"I don't know how to say this without sounding mean, Alice, but if you're just *interested*, then you're not playing on my level."

"I haven't played at all," she said, throwing up her hands. "But I would, with you. I understand you so much more now. I understand your dominant manner, your intensity, the way you talk to people—"

"You don't understand anything." I sounded harsh, but I couldn't soften the words I was saying. "I've been doing this shit for years, and participated in 'scenes' you couldn't even begin to imagine. I go to a club that's for experienced players. I like things you wouldn't like. No, I know you wouldn't like them," I added, when she opened her mouth to speak. I got out of the bed, my erection disappeared from sheer angst. "You should go to bed." I guided her toward my door. Her bare arm felt warm and soft under my palm as I urged her along. "We're both going to forget that you went into my dungeon, and that we had this conversation."

"But...if this is the reason we can't be together..."

"Alice."

"You kissed me once. We made out. Your body told me you wanted me." Tears formed in her eyes, even as she stubbornly set her teeth. "You kissed me like you loved me. I don't understand why this has to stand between us. Love overcomes everything."

Damn it. I couldn't deal with her tears. I took her face in my hands. "Love can't overcome this. Don't you get it? I don't want to hurt you."

"But I want you to hurt me. Hurt me!" Her voice had risen to a cry, her tears spilling over. "What you're into—it can't hurt any worse than never having you when I love you so much."

She didn't get it. She didn't understand, but she wasn't going to leave it alone, and I wanted to fuck her every minute of every day.

Fine. I'd fuck her, just once, just to release the sexual tension that had built up between us. I'd let her "have me," so she could get over it, but I wouldn't hurt her. I'd control myself, and she'd see that I was a man like any other, that pining after me wasn't worth her tears.

No, that's a horrible idea. Send her to her own room. Don't fuck her.

It was too late. My fingers drove into her hair, messing up her pretty little braids. I pressed against her in the doorway, my hot skin cooled by her virginal white nightgown. Blue slunk away down the hall, to his bed in the living room, because he always ran away from things that unsettled him.

"You want me, don't you?" she asked in a small voice, searching my gaze.

"I want you too damn much." I meant it as a warning. For emphasis, I pressed my swollen cock against her belly, hard, but she wasn't deterred. I needed someone to step in and stop me, right now, but there was no one but us, and I was lost in the scent and feel of her body.

"This is such a bad idea," I said, fingering the hem of her cotton nightie. "A horrible idea. We shouldn't do this."

"We were always going to do this."

"Damn you." I inched her nightgown up, running my fingers over the tops of her thighs. As long as I stayed in control, I could go slow, treat her like a lady, all that shit she'd expect from me.

"We're not going to my dungeon," I ground out. "We're not doing any BDSM shit."

She gave me a look that said, *oh, really*, because I was already pressing her against the doorjamb with too much force. "Just take me," she said. "That's what I want."

Fine. I was going to take her. She wanted it, I wanted it, and my bed was just a few footsteps away. She started to pull off her nightgown, but I stopped her.

"Come here. Come with me." She looked at me in confusion as I dragged her toward the bed. "I want you to leave it on, because I don't want to go too fast."

"I want you to go fast."

I pulled her against me and pressed a finger over her lips. "You'd better fucking behave."

Already, as I held her, I had one of her arms twisted behind her back in some instinctive urge to control. She pressed into me, her gorgeous tits rubbing against my chest. I willed the monster inside me to calmness and released her long enough to guide her back onto the bed. My cock was ablaze. Fuck, I needed a condom. Too many days of foreplay had me ready to fall on her and impale her, thrusting like a beast.

No, I needed this to last longer.

I needed her naked.

I needed to be inside her, gentle and slow.

Her nightgown had buttons at the top, and I started undoing them with gritted teeth. She stroked my face, tracing a finger along my jaw. I shuddered, hovering over her, my heavy cock barely contained by my boxers. When these barriers were gone, I'd shove inside her. Excitement choked me, undoing my self-control, muting my internal warnings. I pulled the nightie over her head and threw it away, and slipped a hand down her panties. White panties with little pink hearts. They were gone as soon as I touched them, shoved down her legs.

That was me shoving them down, ripping them, yanking her legs apart to get at her secret core. I tasted her first, dipping my head to drag my tongue along her center. Oh God, the taste of her, after all this time. She arched, grabbing my hair as I sucked on her clit. Too much? Too rough? She groaned and planted her feet on my bed, letting me have her. She tasted like joy and energy, and all the forbidden fantasies I'd locked out of my mind.

I crooked an arm around one of her thighs so she couldn't close her legs, even when I moved away to explore other parts of her. I kissed up her stomach, her soft, sweet belly, and then her breasts with taut, rounded nipples. I wanted to bite her and mark her, pinch those nipples until she screamed and begged me to stop. *No, no, no...* I kissed her shoulder blades and traced her neck with my tongue. She moved her head back, away from me, sighing, and I realized the hand that wasn't holding her leg was wrapped around her neck, squeezing too hard. My hand, choking her.

But she wasn't pulling away. I felt a terrifying rush of dominant adrenaline, felt a little more of my control ebb away. Her hips undulated against me, inviting me to take her. Her fingers traced my waistband, tugging at my boxers. I let go of her leg and pinned her with my body instead, grinding against her hot, damp center with the head of my cock encased in thin cotton. Already, the sensation was too much.

I'd felt close to her so many times. When we made music, when we ate and laughed together, when I'd held her after her apartment disaster, but none of those times was anything like this. I felt transformed by desire, blinded, shocked at how much I wanted her.

How much I wanted to *hurt her.*

I pulled away with a gasp. "Wait."

She clutched at me. "What?"

"Just…give me a minute. I don't want to go too fast." I clenched my teeth from the effort of staying in control. "Okay. Protection. I have a condom in the…the drawer."

I kicked off my boxers and reached to get a rubber, hating the feeling of being apart from her. I rolled on the condom by sheer force of will, the will to protect her, because what I really wanted was to come inside her with nothing between us. I wanted everything. All of her.

I studied her to be sure this was what she wanted, although I was afraid, at this point, it would be impossible for me to stop. Her eyes were glued to my cock, which was engorged and jutting and so fucking hard it hurt.

"You're big," she said.

For the first time, she looked as if her courage might falter. *Yes, I'm big. I'm mean. I'm bad and rough. That's why I tried to say no to you, say no to this.* "We don't have to do this," I said, breathless with lust for her. "We probably shouldn't do this."

She opened her arms to me in answer. Instead of hugging her, I grasped her forearms and pressed them to the bed like the forceful, dominant animal I was. Had I imagined I could control myself, keep the lid on these urges, when she was the woman I'd always wanted most in my life? I parted her legs with my knees, spread them wide so she had no way to stop me as I pressed inside her.

Stop me. Tell me to stop.

She held my gaze and bared her teeth, taking my girth without complaint, my braided, brazen Nordic princess. She was so wet and tight. I died as I eased inside her, holding her arms so hard I probably bruised her. I didn't want her to move, because that might make me fall apart. The whole fucking world spun around me, but I couldn't let her move, because I was only just driving inside her and it was already the best sex I'd ever had. Her walls gripped me, triggering every nerve ending in my dick. She whined, a soft animal whine, and I was about to lose it again.

"No," I said as she arched against me. "I'll hurt you."

She spread her legs wider and whispered, "I want you to hurt me."

And that was the end of all my control.

CHAPTER TEN:
ALICE

I could hardly think. I could barely breathe. My hands made fists as Milo thrust deep inside me, stretching me, driving to the hilt.

Don't let go of me, please, don't let go, don't let go...

No, he wasn't letting go. He held me down with his hands and his body, making me take the thickest cock I'd seen in my life—even in porn—deep inside my pussy. No apologies, no restraint, but I didn't care. When I squirmed to accommodate him, his legs forced mine wider, and his thrusts jarred me, lifting me from the bed. My clit throbbed each time he entered me, and some hyper-stimulated spot inside my walls made me shudder. Sex wasn't supposed to feel this wild and crazy—or maybe it was, and I just never knew it.

Was it this crazy because we'd waited so long? Was that why our joining felt like something happening on some elevated plane? His body covered mine, muscular and hard, commanding, frightening, so wonderfully frightening. Our hips rocked together, and every time he entered me and left me, there was a greater shock of pleasure. I was building to a frantic climax, but it was too soon to come yet.

I struggled against him, like that might hold off the explosion inside me, but I was too far gone. My orgasm came so hard and fast that I couldn't even cry out. I gasped as my pussy walls clenched around his shaft, as wave after wave of pleasure drowned my senses. He slowed, pressing hard in me as the ripples strung out.

"Look at me," he said through clenched teeth. "Look at me while you're coming."

I stared into his dark eyes, which only increased my climax's intensity. I knew him so well, I could read all his feelings—excitement, pleasure, pride. As soon as the orgasm ebbed enough for me to speak, I said, "I came too soon. I wanted more."

"Oh, you're going to get more." He drew out of me in a long, slow slide, maximizing the friction, then pushed in just as slow. Now that the frenzy of my first orgasm had passed, I was able to focus on details I'd missed before, like the feel of his flexing abs against my stomach, and the sensual way he parted his lips.

"Are you ever going to kiss me?" I whispered, looking at those lips.

"Jesus Christ."

He lowered his mouth to mine and kissed me hard, and now that my hands were free, I kissed him back, feeling our connectedness, not just physically, but emotionally. His lips played over mine, his tongue darting between my teeth as his cock throbbed inside me. He was so forcefully erotic, but it felt like the most natural thing in the world, because I'd always known he was like this. I might not have known the particulars, but I knew the general gist.

Hurt me, I thought, when he grabbed a handful of my hair. My braids were in tatters, and he pulled out the elastics so the rest of them would come loose. He wasn't gentle about it either, and I loved that. He yanked back my head, pressing his lips to my neck, and then kissed me again on the mouth, hard, harder, biting my lips. I couldn't breathe because of all the passion, all the violence. No, I couldn't breathe because he was choking me, squeezing my neck. When I realized it, I looked at him in a panic, and he let me go.

"I'm sorry," he said, a breathless gasp. "I'm not going to hurt you."

"Let's go to your dungeon. Please."

"No. Absolutely not."

He was still inside me, looking down at me with a strange, fond kind of dread. He pulled out and made me turn over. I fumbled, heavy with passion, not wanting to lose our connection. He slapped my ass when I looked back over my shoulder, then put his hands on my hips.

All I wanted was to please him, to be in the right position to satisfy him, so when he pulled me into the stance he liked, I didn't care that his fingers left dots of pain behind. My ass cheek felt hot where he'd slapped it, and I wondered what it would be like to feel more—to feel one of the scary implements in his dungeon, the straps or paddles or whips, while I was tied to one of those racks.

He thrust inside me again, holding my hips in his huge hands. His thumbs dug into my ass cheeks and stayed there, too close to my asshole for comfort. If some other guy did that to me, I would have turned over, disentangled myself and said, *no thanks, this isn't for me.* But with Milo, I waited to see what he would do, if he would fondle me there, or press a finger inside, or put his cock there...

God, no, that wouldn't be possible. Would it? I hated the idea, but I also wanted him to do it, to make me take it.

But he'd said he wouldn't hurt me. His cock felt too good again, too wonderful. My hair fell down in my face, obscuring my vision, as he banged into me from behind. One of his hands left my hip and the fingers latched onto my nipple instead, squeezing hard, causing excruciating pain.

I cried out, but it wasn't a pained cry. It was a sex cry. I put my hand over his, tilting off balance. I fell onto my stomach and he fell over me, thrusting even deeper now that I was pinned. My other breast was grabbed and pinched until my nipple ached. My lips fell open, not to beg for mercy, but to let out broken sobs. Even as he hurt me, I shoved my hips back against him with more force. The harder he pinched my nipples, the harder I fucked my pussy on his cock.

"You like when I hurt you," he said, and it wasn't a question. His growl rumbled in my ear, and then he bit my earlobe. I squirmed under him, unmoored from any sense of reality.

"Please, more," I begged. "Hurt me more."

"No."

"Please. I want it."

He grasped my neck, not choking me this time, but holding me on the edge, so I couldn't move without him letting me. His other hand doubled my hair over in his fist as he banged into me. "Come for me, if you like this," he ordered. "Come again on my cock, harder this time."

I felt his teeth latch onto my ear, felt the same sense of panic and surrender that any prey might feel when cornered by a predator. The adrenaline was there too, pushing me into a second orgasm as his cock plundered me, turning me inside out.

"Yes, yes," I cried, squeezing on his length as he tightened his grip on my hair. "I can't..."

I can't bear it. I can't survive this. I can't stop coming when you're inside me.

He let out a ragged breath and drove deep, bracing his knees on the bed between mine. He let go of my neck and hair and pulled at me instead, cinching his arms around my waist so I couldn't escape his final thrusts, no matter how hard and brutal they were. I arched my back, letting him drive even deeper before he finished his orgasm and fell still.

He lay on top of me for a few moments, braced on his elbows. His long hair tickled my back as he placed kisses between my shoulder blades. Although I was exhausted, my pussy still gripped him, unwilling to let our connection end.

"Don't move," he said in a low, jagged growl. "Don't get me started again."

"I don't mind if you get started again."

"Hush." He sounded angry, as angry as he'd been about me trespassing in his dungeon, but he also stroked me gently, smoothing my hair where he'd fisted it into knots. "I didn't want this, Alice. It's not going to end well."

I started to move. He muffled a curse and reached down to pull out, taking care with the condom. So protective, for all his talk of hurting me. I put my arms around his neck. "Why does it have to end?"

He pressed his cheek against mine so I couldn't look in his eyes. "We can't do this. We shouldn't do this."

But we could. We had. "I want to do more," I said. "Everything, all night. Teach me what you love, and if it's something I don't know, I'll learn how to do it. I know you're a Dominant, Milo, and I want to be your submissive. Just show me what to do."

He closed his eyes, like I was causing him pain. "I told you, no dungeon. No."

"Why not? Please." I knew a thing or two about him from our years of friendship, and I knew more now. He couldn't resist me, not if I really begged him. "Please, pretty please? Just show me a few things. The night is young."

* * * * *

"Don't," he said, when I reached down to pick up my panties before we left his bedroom. "If you're going to come to my dungeon..." His gaze ran over my naked body, burning it with his intensity. "If you go there with me, you're all mine. Nothing between us."

No panties, no clothes. Nothing civilized. That was what he meant. He took my hand and dragged me down the hall, the sheen of anger still on him, along with power and desire. Now that we were actually going to his dungeon, he was letting a little more of his dominant side out. He'd looked over my body with an attitude of ownership, and Jesus, the way that made me feel...

91

Alice, babes, do you have any idea what you're getting into?

No, I didn't. I couldn't think about that, or I'd lose my nerve. When Milo ushered me through the forbidden door, Blue hung back, then disappeared down the hallway, declining to come in.

"He's not allowed in here," said Milo, as we watched him go. "You shouldn't be, either."

"I'm sure you'll take care of me."

He pursed his lips and turned on a few of the lights, then told me, "Stay." He moved farther into the silent chamber of furniture and racks while I stared at his naked body. Scary, that he looked bigger and more daunting with his clothes off than on. His cock was a big part of it. Even half-hard, it looked formidable.

He stopped by the pair of cuffs hanging down from the ceiling in the middle of the dungeon. "Come here. This is as good a place to start as any."

To start. A start implied a continuation. Well, if I survived this. I was kind of disappointed I wasn't going to be more tied down, like on the padded bench or the X-shaped rack, but he was the one in charge.

"Raise your hands," he said in a gruff voice that already had my pussy flowing. He buckled my wrists into the cuffs, not looking in my eyes, although I watched his expression for any change in his features. If he was nervous, like me, he didn't show it. *Of course he's not showing it. You're new to this, but he's done it a thousand times.*

He stood back when my hands were bound in the air, and I did see a bit of worry in his features. Worry *and* lust. He circled me as my toes shifted on the smooth wood floor. "How does that feel?" he asked.

I thought a moment. "Scary, but good."

"What now? Do you want me to beat you? Make you cry?"

I sucked in a breath. "I don't know. Do what you like. What you usually do."

"What if you hate what I usually do?" I felt his touch at my back and I flinched. "What if you hate it and you can't get away?"

I shook my head, trembling at his closeness. "I don't know."

"If you hate it, you use a safe word."

Oh yes, I remembered reading about safe words while I waited for him to come home. BDSM culture was very big on safe words.

I turned to look at him, wanting to curl myself against him, but he stood rigidly away from me, his cock erect. "What safe word should I use?" I asked.

"Lala," he said, like he'd already thought about it. "As many times as it takes to make me stop. Lala lala lala lala lala, like you're singing. I know you hate that name."

"Yes, I do. I'll never use it."

"Brave words," he said, raising an eyebrow. Finally, he came close enough to touch me, tracing fingers down my cheeks and across my chin. "This would be enough for me, you know. Seeing you like this, bound and scared."

I bit my lip. "I'm not sure if it's enough for me."

"You've never done anything like this?" he asked, although I'd already confessed my ignorance.

"It's all new," I said in a soft voice. "But I'm ready."

He leaned in and kissed me, his hands cupping my breasts. His cock poked against my belly and I felt another wave of arousal between my legs. All too soon, he broke the kiss. "Here are the ground rules when we play," he said. "You don't try to get away from the things I do to you. If it hurts, that's too bad. Understand? Answer '*Yes, Sir.*' In this dungeon, I'm always 'Sir.'"

"Yes, Sir." I was getting so turned on from his words, I was afraid the moisture in my pussy would start running down my leg.

"No asking me to stop. You can cry, scream, or tremble, but no whining or asking for a reprieve. You won't get it."

I swallowed hard. "Yes, Sir."

"In this dungeon, you're mine until you use a safe word." His hand traced down my back and over my ass cheek, then he squeezed a handful of it. "Your ass is mine," he said. He slapped one of my breasts, and I gasped. "Your tits are mine. Open your mouth." I did, and he thrust a finger inside it. "Your mouth is mine. Your lips are mine, your tongue is mine. Got it?"

"Yes, Sir," I said around his finger in garbled agreement. He removed his finger, but our gazes stayed locked.

"Are you ready? You're sure you want this?" he asked, his eyes dangerously intent.

"Yes, Sir." *Please fuck me. Oh God, I'm about to die here.* "Yes, please, Sir."

He broke our stare-down and walked over to the cabinets along the wall, returning with a pair of silver clamps. He slapped my left breast, then my right. I flinched, unused to so much sensation. So much *roughness*. After he slapped them both a couple times, he yanked on my nipples. They were hard from fear more than anything, and he pinched them and twisted them, then clamped them, one after the other. The whole process took a few seconds, but the pain...

"Oh God," I whispered. No begging, no whining, no entreating him to take them off. *If it hurts, that's too bad.* He moved back to the cabinets, leaving the silver clips dangling from my nipples, causing cascades of pain to shoot through my breasts. I gritted my teeth as he opened a drawer, removing a thin, supple strap with a handle.

Okay, okay, you're okay. I breathed through my teeth, preparing myself. It wasn't that big of an implement. He wasn't going to break anything, well, aside from my nipples, which throbbed from the clamps. He moved behind me.

"Spread your legs," he instructed. "Spread them as wide as you can, so you can brace yourself. I don't want any hopping or turning around."

"Yes, Sir." My voice quavered. My legs trembled as I inched them apart.

"Wider," he said impatiently.

I spread them as wide as I could with my arms stretched over me. The first lick of the strap caught me by surprise. It wasn't unbearable, no, but it stung like hell, and I jumped and twisted sideways.

"Nope," he said, turning me back again. "I was going to start you out with five, but you just earned five more. I'll say it again. No turning or hopping. Keep your feet flat on the ground. You said you wanted this."

Yes, I had. I could keep my feet still if I tried. I really wanted to try.

"Spread your legs the way you're supposed to, Alice, and behave this time," he said. "You have nine more, if you're good."

Nine sounded like plenty., I braced to be still, and when the next stinging blow came, I curled my toes, but didn't move them.

"That's better," he said. The positive feedback was nice, but my nipples were killing me and I had eight more strap strokes to go. I reached my hands around to grasp the chains above me. Each stroke he dealt was successively harder, but the threat of more pain kept my feet rooted to the floor, even when my body's natural impulse was to try to escape the stinging punishment. *Six. Seven. Eight.* I counted them in my head as he doled them out in a controlled, steady stream. Nine hit me right between the cheeks. *Oww.* Ten was the hardest of all, and I jumped.

"That's five more," he said.

Shit, shit, shit. I tensed my body—and my butt cheeks—so I wouldn't jump my way up to twenty. Or twenty-five. Or thirty. Just thinking about it made me want to cry. My ass burned from the first ten strokes. How long had it been since he started on me? Two minutes? Three? Could I take five more licks? Would this scene go on for half an hour? An hour? How much pain could I take?

I felt his hand on my neck, then in my hair, grasping it and giving me a little shake. "Your ass is mine, remember? Your body is mine. All you have to do is let it happen."

Let it happen. Give your body to him, your stinging ass cheeks and your smarting nipples. He owns you right now. He was making that perfectly clear. There was no tenderness in this Milo, no protectiveness. This pain was what he'd been trying to protect me from—he clearly enjoyed doling it out.

"I'm trying to be still," I said on a sob.

"Then be still."

He let go of my hair, and another strap stroke lit my ass on fire. I wanted to turn and look over my shoulder. Just looking at him would have calmed me, but I wasn't allowed to turn around. I realized now that this kind of bondage was much worse than a spanking bench or a rack, where I'd be tied so I couldn't turn or move, even if I wanted to.

Then I realized why we were starting this way. Because taking the pain had to be my choice. I had to stand here and endure it on my own steam, without anything holding me down.

After that, I had no problems standing still, even if my ass cheeks still clenched with each merciless lick. I was proud of myself, but my only reward was to have the nipple clamps removed—which caused a great deal of pain in itself. He placed them on a nearby table, then reached over my head to release my cuffed wrists from the chains. I wondered for a moment if we were done, but he wasn't acting like we were done.

"Stretch your arms for a moment, then put your hands behind you," he said shortly.

I obeyed, getting the circulation flowing with a few arm and shoulder rolls, then reaching behind me where he waited. He took my wrists in firm fingers, and a couple clicks later, my arms were bound behind me in cuffs.

"Are you having fun?" he asked, his lips against my ear.

What else could I say? "Yes, Sir."

He gave a soft laugh and nudged me forward onto my knees. I went down, my hurting, strapped ass cheeks feeling exposed and vulnerable. I tried to soothe them with my palms as I knelt, but Milo grabbed the cuffs and gave me a rough rattle of control.

"Don't try to rub the sting away. I prefer you hurting. I'm a sadist, that's what I've been trying to explain to you. I'm not satisfied if you're not in pain. Keep your hands at the small of your back."

He came to stand in front of me, and used my hair to position me to his liking. He ripped opened a condom; a fruity scent filled my nostrils as he rolled the flavored rubber onto his massive cock. "Open your mouth," he said.

I did, thinking there was no way he was going to fit inside it. He was just too big.

"No, *open your mouth*," he scolded. "Like, to suck a fucking cock."

He put his thumbs at the corners of my jaw and pressed my mouth open until it was gaping. Then he eased inside, depressing my tongue with his shaft. I gagged, trying to take him deeper, but he could only get so far.

"Calm down." His voice was cool with an edge of menace. "Do what you can."

He didn't leave me much choice. He held my head as he thrust into my mouth, making me take more than I thought I could. Each time he pressed forward, I choked, and each time he pulled back, another tear spilled down my cheeks.

"Out of practice, or you've only sucked tiny cocks?" he taunted. "You wanted this, Alice, you asked for it. You say you want what I'm into? This is what I'm into. Choking you on my cock until you cry."

I stared up at him. *Yes, I want this. I still love you. You're making me feel like the most sexual, wild creature in the world.*

"Do you want me to stop?" he asked, pulling out. "Had enough?"

I shook my head, sucking up the drool that had collected on my chest. "I want you to hurt me. Fuck me again, hard." I didn't know where the words came from. Maybe I knew he wanted me to say them. My pussy was dripping from pain and fear, and being used for his pleasure. His force brought me more pleasure than any other lover had brought me. I didn't know how that worked, it just did. "Please, please, Sir," I said. Did that count as begging?

He crouched beside me and shoved me forward, holding my bound wrists so I couldn't get away. I didn't want to get away. I wanted him to hold me down and ravage me. "Don't fucking move," he said. "No, keep your mouth open, in case I want to fuck it again."

While he spoke, he crossed to get a bottle of lube from the cabinet. When he returned, he moved it in front of my face. "Know what this is for, my stubborn masochist?" he asked.

Wow. Oh my God. No, you won't get in. "Yes, Sir," I managed to say aloud.

"Tell me. Say it out loud, Alice. What's this for, in general usage?"

"Anal sex." My throat closed up with nerves.

"Louder."

"Anal sex," I repeated,

"Assfucking," he corrected me with a lurid tilt to his lips. "So, Alice, ask me to fuck your ass."

"Please, Sir, please fuck my ass," I said, although the idea of it terrified me. My cheeks were still sore from the strapping, and my sensitive nipples rubbed against the floor as he held my wrists behind my back.

"Do you really want me to?"

My gaze strayed from his eyes to his broad, bronze shoulders, then down his hard abs, and finally to his jutting cock. "I want what you want, Sir."

He laughed. "Good answer."

He positioned himself behind me, his cock sliding between my folds, then into my dripping pussy. I let out a breath I hadn't known I was holding. He'd been testing me again, seeing if I'd *really* do anything.

But he fucked my pussy instead of my asshole, bringing the familiar stretch and pleasure, which was magnified by the fact that I couldn't move my arms. I was his captive, his sex slave. His submissive. I understood why people loved this. There was something about giving all your power to another person, for their pleasure, so you could be used. My body responded to his dominance with an almost painful level of arousal. This was why I'd been drawn to him all those years, why my sex organs went into overdrive whenever he was around.

"Oh, yes, please," I said, as my orgasm crept closer. The clamps, the strapping, the cuffs, all of it had led to this wild fucking. "I need more, please, Sir."

Milo made a rough sound and pulled out of me. I arched my hips, wanting him back again, but then I heard the *snick* of the lube's cap. He groped between my ass cheeks, depositing slickness around my tiny hole. I clenched it shut as his finger pressed some of the lube inside. He answered this protective impulse with a chuckle.

"Don't worry, naughty girl. This lube will let anything slide in there."

He probed me again with his finger, driving it deep inside my ass, making me question my sanity. *Lala. Say Lala, because it's time for that safe word.* My lips parted to say the word, but then he grasped my cuffs again, positioning himself behind me, and I felt trapped and horny, overcome with desire. *Please, Sir, I want you to fuck my ass. Please, Sir, just don't hurt me.*

I repeated it in my mind as he parted my ass cheeks and pushed the head of his cock against my hole. I made a small, panicked sound as he started stretching me open with the tip. *You'll never fit. You'll break me. I've never, ever done this before.* He was breaching my hole, inch by inch, hurting me just as I'd asked to be hurt. "Oh God, oh God, oh God," I whispered, pressing my face against the floor. He held me tightly, redoubling his hold on my cuffs.

"Relax," he said. "Let me in."

I moved my hips, trying to accustom myself to the awful stretching sensation. His fingers stroked my clit, presumably to "relax" me, but it was hard to process anything aside from the burning ache of his entry. I knew if I said *Lala* he would stop, that everything would stop. The hurting, the forcing, the thrilling pleasure that was making me fall apart.

But I couldn't tell him to stop. He kneaded my hips and eased forward, inch by inch, fucking me in a place I'd never been fucked before. "Oh God," I whined, because I wasn't sure I could take much more. He was going slow, easing his way forward with the lube's help, but he was so big.

Then my tensing asshole relaxed, and a little of the ache ebbed away. It was replaced by pure pressure and fullness, a feeling like nothing I'd ever experienced. He went still for a moment, making small movements in and out of my ass. I was utterly impaled, and under his control.

"Please, Sir, I..." I didn't know what I wanted, or why I kept saying *please*, only knew that he would make this all make sense.

"Does it hurt?" he asked in a rough-edged voice.

I made a small moaning sound.

He pressed even deeper, drawing a breath against my ear. "You wanted to be hurt," he murmured. "Does it hurt, baby? Answer me."

"Yes."

"Do you like the way it hurts?"

"Oh, yes, Sir. Yes, I like it."

"You want me to really fuck your ass now?"

"Yes, please." It was what I'd been begging for all along, this ultimate intrusion and debasement. Now that my asshole had stretched to his full girth, the lube made it easy for him to slide.

"Arch your hips back," he said in a voice like a patient teacher. "Show me how much you want it."

Arching my hips brought new sensations as he withdrew, then surged into me again. Just when I got used to that, he pulled my hair with a sharp tug, causing me to tense. Sometimes he pinched my nipples as he drove in and out, adding pain on top of pain as I trembled under him. When I tried to twist away from his grasp, he paused deep inside me and shook the cuffs, guiding them higher on my back. He forced my fisted hands open.

"Leave your hands open until I'm done."

I shivered at the edge in his voice, and stretched my fingers apart, fighting the urge to clench them closed again with each thrust. This was another test, like keeping my feet on the ground while he strapped me. It was another layer of control, like he didn't already have enough control over me. His fingers tightened on the cuffs, holding me in position whenever I squirmed forward or sideways. He grabbed my hair if I moved my head, twisting it hard.

Ow, ow, ow, my hair, my asshole, oh God, please don't stop. I curled my toes since I couldn't clench my fingers. Milo pressed his cheek to mine, rough stubble and a hard, thrusting body above me. I gave an endless cry, a broken whine of submission, and his teeth closed on my ear.

I bucked, wishing I could rub my clit. I was desperate to come with him deep inside my ass, but I knew I couldn't. I moved my hips anyway, and he slid a hand beneath me to part my pussy lips and pinch my clit the same way he'd pinched my nipples, to the point of excruciating pain.

I threw my head back and came, my asshole squeezing around him as he fucked me to oblivion. My fingers clenched so hard they felt numb and frozen, but the rest of me was on fire. After a few hard thrusts he pushed deep, went still, and shuddered violently. I squeezed his cock until he groaned, then I rode out my climax a few more moments, until it faded, leaving me limp and breathless.

His fingers relaxed in my hair. One of his hands returned to my nipple, giving a last, long, leisurely pinch. I felt it in my clit. His cock moved in my ass, and just like that, I wanted more. I wanted him again. What was wrong with me? What was he doing to me? I could barely lift my head.

"Again," I said. "Please, all of it again."

"No, Alice. This has to be it." He pulled out of me, rolling onto his back. "I've done enough to you. We can't go any further than this."

"Please."

He sat up and cupped my face in one large hand, his gaze afire. "You don't understand. This is as much as I can responsibly do to you, because you're a beginner."

"I'm not a beginner anymore, and I didn't use the safe word," I protested, making my case. "I didn't come close, even once."

He muttered a scathing stream of profanities, then tightened his fingers on my chin, kissing me ruthlessly until I had to struggle up for air. "Once more," he said. "That's it. No more after that."

CHAPTER ELEVEN: MILO

I woke around ten, with Alice dead to the world beside me. Either that, or she was playing dead so she wouldn't have to face me in the daylight, a definite possibility after the things I'd done to her last night.

Blue stood beside the bed—her side—looking delighted to find us together. His nose almost, but not quite, rested on her opened hand.

"She's sleeping," I mouthed. And then, "Don't get your hopes up."

Blue loved Alice as much as I did. Well, that wasn't possible, because I loved her more than anything, but Blue came in a close second, maybe tied with her mom and dad. And my mom and dad. Hell, everyone loved Alice, and I'd used and abused her body like a fucking animal for hours last night. Not okay.

Just once, I'd told myself. Ha. We'd ended up in my dungeon fucking a second and third time, after all my protests that I'd never take her there. Then we'd showered, had a 2 a.m. snack, and fucked again in her bedroom when I'd gone in there intending to make her sleep.

I did finally get her to sleep, until around four a.m., when she crawled into my bed and snuggled beside me. Yep, more sex. In the wee hours of the night, I was straddling her face and fucking her throat, and she was gazing up at me, crying and gagging, telling me everything was okay. Her mouth felt like heaven, that was my only excuse for not stopping, because everything was *not* okay.

I'd acted like a fucking jerk, taking everything I could from her once the floodgates had opened. Never mind that I had to look her in the eyes this morning, with her *knowing*. Knowing the depths of my lust, as well as the heights of my depravity. Well, the lower heights. If my perversity was a twenty-story building, I'd taken her to somewhere between the third and fourth floor.

So much for self-control, for not hurting her. Fuck.

I slid out of bed and went into the bathroom, and stared at myself in the mirror. Was I that terrible a person? There was nothing I'd done that she hadn't consented to. I'd gone easy with the strap, used my least painful clamps, and limited the number of times I'd gagged her on my cock. I'd only grabbed her neck three...maybe four...times, and I'd used more than enough lube when I fucked her ass. I'd also monitored her the entire time to be sure she was as turned on as I was. I'd protected her, to an extent.

And she, the white-nightied siren, had done nothing to convince me to put on the brakes. No, she was as hot and willing at four in the morning as she'd been when I ripped off her panties the night before. She'd told me, with a straight face, *I'm not a beginner anymore.* I hadn't contradicted her, because she looked so proud of herself. I might have said a few swear words.

I turned on the shower and stood under the water, wondering what to do now. Maybe I should give the fuck up and marry her. If she was my wife, maybe I'd find the basic couth and control I hadn't been able to find last night. As hot water slid down my back and chest, I allowed myself a few moments of daydreaming: Alice in a frothy white wedding dress, both sets of our parents smiling as we walked down the aisle. An erotically charged newlywed life, then later, children and closeness and family concerts by the fire.

Nice daydream. But what about the nightmare, when I asked her to go with me to The Gallery? I wasn't sure I could hurt, really torment, someone I was in love with, which was why I'd never fallen in love with any of my other subs.

Now I was in love, and Alice had subbed to me, eating up the pain like candy. Had she really enjoyed it, or had she swallowed it down because she loved me? How much would she agree to before it became too much? Would she let me torture other subs at The Gallery, and give herself over to other men, per the rules? Could I let her, without losing my shit completely? My daydreams of marital bliss were replaced by nightmares of divorce and custody proceedings, if not charges of spousal abuse.

I shut off the water, shutting down my thoughts on that topic at the same time. No, never abuse—but what if she saw it that way? Despite what she believed, she was an absolute beginner.

An absolute beginner who was still fast asleep in my bed.

I threw on a tee and some jeans, and went out to the kitchen to start some coffee. It was a dreary winter day, the skies threatening snow. I heard Alice in the shower about half an hour later. While I sat at the table, Blue paced up and down the hall, trying to be with both of us at once. By the time she emerged, he couldn't wait to press against her side.

"Good morning, sweet friend," she said to him, providing the demanded attention. Then she glanced up at me, and it took all my strength not to look away. All the things I'd done to her the night before flashed through my mind, and while part of me was ashamed, part of me wanted to do them all over again.

"Want some coffee?" I asked. *And I'm sorry.*

And I want you again.

She came to join me at the table, blushing, sexy, lovely Alice. Hell. Fuck. Why wasn't she telling me I was a pervert and a creep, and to leave her the fuck alone in the future? Nope, she seemed happy to see me. I stood to embrace her, kissing the top of her head, because if I kissed her lips I'd lose it. "How are you this morning?" I murmured.

She shook her head and snuggled closer to me. "I can't even explain."

I can't even explain summed up my feelings as well, but someone had to say something about the shit we'd done last night. I guided her into a chair, then returned to the kitchen, putting together words as I poured her some coffee. Her favorite type of breakfast cereal—dry—was already in a bowl in front of her.

"So," I said, returning with her cup. "We got pretty wild last night. Wilder than I meant to get."

"That was probably my fault. I was the one who came to your room last night, and I think deep inside I wanted..."

"To seduce me? You were successful." I watched as she stirred sugar into her coffee. "The question is, how do you feel about it this morning?"

"I feel fine," she said quickly. "I'm a little tired, but...well...I wouldn't give up any of what we did last night." She looked at me from under her lashes. "Or what we did this morning."

I leaned back in my chair, wondering how to proceed. I wouldn't give up any of what we did either, but I also needed her to realize it had been a one-time thing, a grievous lapse in my self-control.

"You know—" I began, meaning to say something about preserving the sanctity of our friendship, while apologizing for treating her with so little respect.

"I can't wait to do some more BDSM stuff," she said, speaking over me. "I shouldn't have barged into your room last night and put you on the spot about your dungeon and everything, but I was so fascinated, and when you took me in there and..." She grinned as a blush crept up her cheeks. "It was so much scarier and cooler and amazing than I could have dreamed."

She tugged at a lock of her soft ginger hair. All I could think about was the way I'd wrenched it in my fist. I could practically feel the soft strands against my skin.

"The thing is, Alice—"

"I know, I know. You're more experienced than me, but I don't mind learning what you like." Her blush deepened as she stared at my hands, then met my eyes again. "It's like, all these years I've been having sex, and it was gentle and nice and mostly fulfilling, but until last night, I didn't realize how much more could happen between people. A *lot* happened between us."

"I know." I nodded, biting my tongue. "But maybe..." *Maybe too much happened. Maybe this is a dangerous line we're about to cross.*

"You think I'm this innocent," Alice said, keeping her voice light. "Even last night, I could see on your face that you thought you were being too mean to me."

"I wasn't being mean."

"I know, it's your sadism thing."

"I wasn't being mean," I repeated, willing her to listen. "That violence is how I express passion. I get off on causing anxiety and pain, so a lot of the time, I'm too rough."

"I didn't stop you. If it was too much, I would have used the safe word. Honestly, when you were tying me up, I wanted to die from excitement. And what you did after... I mean, it hurt, but it felt good at the same time. It felt thrilling. Everything in my body was buzzing."

I drained the rest of my coffee, giving up the argument for now. She had stars in her eyes. She wanted more, and it would be so easy for her to convince me to give her more.

"You know, there's a BDSM club in this area that's really popular. I saw it online. It's called Underworld."

Underworld? My God.

"Maybe we could go there together." She ducked her head, my little innocent. "I mean, you've probably been there already."

"I have."

She looked delighted. I closed my eyes a moment, wondering how to tell her that I'd outgrown the play scenes at Underworld in my teens. For a moment, the crunching of her dry cereal was the only sound between us. I had to end this before her blush got any pinker, before she got any more excited about going to Underworld.

"I don't want to disappoint you, because I love you so much, Alice, but we're not doing any more BDSM together."

"What do you mean?"

"It's too dangerous. I'm afraid you don't really understand the sexual sadism thing."

"I understand it fine." She frowned, huffing out a breath. "We had such a great time last night. What am I missing? Am I crazy?"

"I told you last night that we weren't going to go any further," I reminded her.

"And then we did, because we couldn't keep our hands off each other. What's the deal? It seems like the more compatibility we find with each other, the more you shove me away."

"Alice…I'm afraid you're making yourself compatible because you want to promote this relationship between us that's never going to work."

"Why won't it work?"

"Because I…I'm not good at relationships." Maybe that was a way to put it that she'd actually understand. "And I don't plan on getting married, ever, so I don't want to lead you on."

"I don't care if we get married. Just because I babbled about it that one time…" She shrugged. "I don't know if I want to get married either. Can't we just have fun?"

"I'm not going to be your fuckbuddy. Jesus. I took advantage of your willingness last night when I shouldn't have. What happened was a mistake, something I didn't intend to do."

Mistake was probably a bad way to phrase it. It definitely upset her, but I was damned either way. If I agreed to keep playing with her, things would eventually become unmanageable. If I insisted on a platonic friendship, I probably wouldn't have a friend. *And if you'd controlled your fucking urges, jackass, you wouldn't be in this situation.* She pushed back her chair, the hurt I'd caused apparent on her features.

"You make me so angry." She didn't stamp her foot, but the voice was classic Lala, blunt, icy, and Nordic. "Friends can become lovers, you know. Friends can fall in love and have crazy, kinky sex, and everything can still be okay."

She was driving me crazy. I wanted to slap her, or spank her, or read her the rules of The Gallery, and ask if she still believed everything would be okay. *Any submissive brought into The Gallery shall be considered communal property and shared in any way her sponsor desires. The Gallery is a no-safe-word zone. The submissive's limits will be determined by her sponsor.* She didn't understand that my idea of crazy, kinky sex was so much crazier and kinkier than anything she could dream up in her BDSM-beginner's brain.

She didn't understand how much I did *not* want to reveal that side of myself to her.

"It's not okay for me to...be with you in that way," I said. "For me, it's not okay. Please try to understand."

The earlier warmth between us, the embrace, the chaste kiss on the top of her head, it all seemed a million miles away. She was furious, and I was a jerk. The passion we'd experienced in our all-night lust explosion had become something negative, a point of contention. I hated that everything was ruined, that she wouldn't be able to look back on our encounter together with any fond memories.

"I'm sorry," I said, spreading my hands in apology. "I want us to stay friends, along with our families. I want to help you whenever I can, and make you that violin."

"I don't want a violin from you anymore." Her lips trembled. Tears welled in her eyes. "I'd just feel sad every time I played it. You're making me really sad, Milo, because you're being weird and prickly, and acting like...acting like you don't like me at all."

"You know that's not true."

"Really?" She passed a hand over her eyes and stalked from the kitchen, through the living room, and down the hall.

"Where are you going?" I asked.

I saw her wipe away a tear as she went into her room. "I'm leaving. I'm not staying here anymore."

I followed her and got in her way. "You don't have to leave. Can't we just go back to how things were before last night? We'll be friends. You can sleep in my guest room. We can hang out with Blue."

She ducked around me and went to her closet for her luggage. "I don't think that's possible now."

I didn't help as she carried out a suitcase. "I don't want you to leave, Alice, not like this." I tried—and failed—to get in her way. "Do you remember what happened last time you left, or nearly left? What almost happened to you?"

"Yes, I remember," she said, throwing her suitcase on the bed. "It's very hard to forget that my apartment exploded. That's why my violin's gone, and all the clothes I liked, and all my shit. I would have exploded too, right? Maybe I should have, so I could have avoided all this embarrassment."

"Don't say things like that. And what embarrassment are you talking about? I'm not rejecting you. I'm trying to protect you."

"You keep saying that, like you're a fucking land mine or something." She threw the contents of her underwear drawer in the suitcase, and added jeans and shirts on top of it. "I'm going to stay in a hotel."

I grabbed her around the waist as she headed back to her closet. "No, you're not."

"You can't stop me." She broke away and started jerking clothes from their hangers. "The insurance will pay for it."

"You're not storming out of here to move into some random hotel, not like this. No."

"Are you going to hold me hostage?"

She glared at me from inside the closet, and for a moment, I thought how fun it would be to hold her hostage, tie her up, put duct tape over her sassy mouth.

Yep, that was why I couldn't be with her. Fuck me. Damn it.

I left her to her angry packing, went over by her door, and opened a window on my phone. She glared at me, throwing clothes into the other new suitcase we'd bought to replace the ones that'd gone up in flames.

"What are you doing?" she snapped.

"Calling Ella to see if you can use her place, the apartment she got through work. She mostly lives with Devin now. Do you think that would work? It's a decent-sized two bedroom on Mercer Street."

"I don't want to move into your friend's apartment. Then you'll know where to find me."

"So our friendship is over forever?" I threw up my hands. "You're going to hide from me, and avoid talking to me ever again?"

"Yes, I would like to," she yelled.

"I think you're overreacting." When I got angsty, more of my Italian accent came out. "Are you that hard up, that you need to be with a soulless sadist like me?"

She shoved down a jumble of clothes and slammed one of the suitcases shut. "It has nothing to do with being hard up. And you're not soulless. Last night, I thought you were even more amazing than I knew. I thought everything felt great. I thought it was perfect."

"Alice." I sighed. "That feeling won't last."

She shook her head and went back to packing. "You're such a fucking asshole."

"Thank you for finally realizing what I've been telling you all along." I looked down at my phone. "Ella says you can use her place. She has the lease for two more months, so she'll meet us there with the keys."

111

Alice opened her mouth to refuse the offer, but my expression must have made her reconsider.

"Fine. That's nice of her," she finally said.

"I'm going to take you there with all your stuff," I said, indicating the pile she'd made of her belongings, "and let you have all the space you want, for as long as you want." I sat at the foot of the bed. She had so few things since the fire, she was almost done packing. "But I'm still making you a violin."

"Great." She closed the other suitcase with a *whump*. "I'll never play it. I'll sell it to someone else for lots of money."

After that, she gave me the silent treatment. Fine. She had a right to be angry, just as I had a right to protect her from my deviant sex life. Someday she'd calm down and forgive me for everything. Maybe in a year or two, we could go back to being something akin to friends. But there would always be that one night between us, and the wretched morning after.

When I returned from taking her to Ella's place, Blue moped around the living room, and finally sprawled with theatrical melancholy in his bed.

"No wonder you got along so well," I told him. "You're both drama queens. Hey, man, you could have tried harder to make her stay." But he'd disappeared when we started arguing, because he hated conflict. I wasn't a fan of it either. "She might come back." *But I doubt it.*

I went into the now-empty guest room, because I already missed her and the energy she'd brought to my quiet place. Everything was arranged the way it had been when she'd first moved in. Maybe she was wise to pack her things and get out. It was too hard for the two of us to live together. She'd taken everything, except the Pressenda violin I'd loaned her, which was propped in its case outside my instrument room's door.

Over the last twenty-four hours, our relationship had gone from the highest emotional highs to the darkest depths, like the greatest violin concertos, only this concerto was unfinished, its denouement cut short.

CHAPTER TWELVE:
ALICE

Ella's loaner apartment was older and charming, like the apartment I'd bought in the Michelin building. Well, the former Michelin building.

I cried as I unpacked, going over everything that had happened between Milo and me. In hindsight, it was so embarrassing. I'd offered myself to him with no reservations, practically begging him for sex. He'd fucked me everywhere, grasping and controlling me, acting out my perfect fantasy of a dominant lover. A *Dominant*, as they said in the lifestyle. Capital D. I'd done things with Milo that I'd never done with anyone else, and now I hurt in places that had never hurt before in my pre-masochistic life.

I'd been so turned on by everything he did. I'd been so excited by his violent possession, so eager to try more. I'd been so sure our night of connection was the start of our "forever" love story, but no. It turns out it was just a tawdry, ill-thought-out one night stand on his end.

Ugh. I had to let it go. Ella's minimalist apartment didn't have a large, cozy fireplace, or a shy greyhound who loved me, or a climate-controlled instrument room, or a secret dungeon, but it was a place to be alone and lick my wounds. Eventually I stopped crying and finished unpacking, and decided I'd make the best of things. I called a fellow violinist from the orchestra, a pompous society son who took every opportunity to brag about his vast collection of instruments. He agreed to let me borrow a modern vintage Yang until I figured out what violin I'd buy next.

A Fierro was out. Milo could make me as many violins as he wanted, but I'd never play any of them. Too much sadness. There were plenty of other contemporary makers I could look into, or maybe I'd spring for a Strad of my own. My father could help me track one down with his network of musical contacts. I emailed him the next day, after a frustrating rehearsal with the Yang, and wrote in English rather than Swedish so he'd be less likely to sense that my life was unraveling.

Dear Pappa,

How are you? I'm doing well. I've found a new place to live while I look for an apartment, courtesy of one of Milo's friends. It's on Mercer Street, in a very busy area of the city, but I like it a lot. Maybe I'll look for something down here in Lower Manhattan, rather than the area around Lincoln Center.

I'm also having second thoughts about playing a Fierro for my next instrument. I was thinking about trying one of the older makers, just for a change? I'm sure there are options to buy here in New York, but maybe you can ask if any of your friends would like to sell. I'm open to anything.

That's it for now. We're playing Tchaikovsky tonight, Orchestral Suite No. 2. Give Mamma a kiss from me. Please visit soon!

Love,

Lilly-Alice

His reply came the next day in Swedish. Yes, he would ask around with his friends, but why not a Fierro violin again? Wasn't Milo making me one? I delayed answering the email, and hoped my dad wouldn't call. It would worry him to know that Milo and I weren't on good terms anymore, especially since proximity to Milo was one of the main reasons I'd taken the job at Met Orchestra.

A few days after I moved in, Ella texted and asked if she could stop by. I couldn't delay that reply, since it was her place, and some of her things were still stashed in the closet. She showed up a few hours later with her friend Juliet.

"Hi, it's good to see you both," I said as I let them in. "But I have a question. Did Milo send you?"

"No," said Ella, blinking her blue eyes. "Well, kind of."

"What she means is that we're here because of Milo," said Juliet. "But he didn't ask us to come."

"Not in so many words," Ella hedged. She looked around the living room, her expression brightening. "It looks like you've mostly moved in."

"I have. Thank you so much for letting me borrow this place."

She shrugged. "I haven't been using it, and I was given an open-ended lease, rent free. The National Science Foundation is footing the bill."

I remembered that Ella was a theoretical astrophysicist, working on some high-level project, and that Juliet managed some rich, famous artist. Not only that, but they were both in happy, healthy relationships. Juliet's engagement ring sparkled as she threaded her fingers around the cuff of her over-the-knee socks. Ella sat on the edge of the couch, looking uncomfortable, even though this was her place.

"Can I get you something to drink?" I asked them.

"That's okay," said Juliet. "We don't want to take up your afternoon. You play with the orchestra tonight, don't you?"

"My call time's not until six."

"Oh, okay." Ella let out a breath and looked at her friend. "So, the reason we're here is that we heard through Fort and Devin that you and Milo had a..."

I waited to see what we'd had. A fling? A one-night stand?

"A falling out," Juliet provided as Ella fell silent. "Milo confided with Fort about what happened between you."

"Not all the details," said Ella quickly, in a way that made me think she knew way too many of the details. "Just that you found his dungeon, and the two of you played in there a little, and that things didn't go well."

"That's the thing," I said, scratching my temple. "They *did* go well, in my mind at least. But he was like, *that's that, we're not doing anything else, I don't want to hurt you, blah blah blah.* So, you know..." I was the one to shrug this time. "I felt like I had to move out, because I couldn't think of him as 'just a friend' after the things that went on."

"Nothing he did upset you?" asked Ella.

"No, I enjoyed all of it. I mean, I guess you know what he's into."

They both nodded, and Ella blushed, biting her lip. "Full disclosure: we're into it too, Alice. The BDSM, the power exchange and sado-masochistic stuff."

"Cause it's fun, right? I really liked all the crazy stuff he did. He bound my hands and spanked me, and used—" I gestured toward my breasts.

"Nipple clamps?" Juliet provided.

"Yes. He even choked me once. Well, a few times. Not real choking, but you know, gripping my neck really hard. He thought it was too much for me, but it wasn't too much at all. It's like he's ashamed of the kinky activities he enjoys."

"I don't know," said Ella. "Maybe he's just worried about letting his sadist flag fly around someone new. Someone...inexperienced."

I tried hard not to roll my eyes. "I guess he's used to playing with more experienced people. I get it, but there's more between us. We have a longtime connection."

Juliet looked down at her ring, straightening it on her finger. "I heard Milo tell Fort that he loved you."

"I guess. Unfortunately, he loves me like a sister. Or a cousin."

"No, it's more than that." She leaned closer, meeting my eyes. "He and Fort talked about you for a long time, and I wasn't supposed to be listening, but I was just so fascinated to hear Milo say that he loved someone, and that he didn't know what to do."

"Because Milo always knows what to do," said Ella.

I looked at them, wishing they'd say what they'd come here to say. The more they talked about Milo, the more I remembered our torrid night, and the worse I felt. "Milo's made up his mind about me," I said. "He 'respects me too much' to take things any further. It was a brutal conversation." I looked around at Ella's mostly bare apartment. "That's why I had to come here. He didn't want me to go to a hotel."

"Because he cares about you," said Juliet.

The women exchanged a look again, Juliet dark-haired, and Ella as blonde as a northern Swede. Then both of them fixed their eyes on me.

"I'm just going to say this." Ella moved closer to where I sat. "Milo Fierro is kind of famous at this club we go to, for being the most hardcore guy."

"A club? Is it Underworld?"

Both of them shook their head. "It's a private club. I can't tell you the name, because that's how private it is, but I can tell you that it's open every Saturday night, and Milo goes a lot."

"Well, he went a lot before you moved in with him," Juliet said. "Not so much the last few weeks. Our friends have been asking about him."

"You go to this club too?"

Ella nodded. "Occasionally. Not so much anymore. It's harder to go when you're in a monogamous relationship, because of the sharing rule."

"The sharing rule?"

Juliet jumped in. "There are five rules for submissives at The G—" She mashed her lips shut. "At this secret club. The first is that you have to be taken there by a sponsor, a Dominant who's a member. You can't just show up. The second rule is that your sponsor can share you with anyone else who's there."

My mouth dropped open. Two rules in, and I was aghast. "You mean, strangers?"

"Sometimes. Most of them you kind of know."

"You guys were shared like that?" When they nodded, a thousand questions sprang to my mind. "What— How—?"

"It's just the way things are there, the bawdy atmosphere. It's a very free place, and everyone shares the same kinks. All the guys are sadist Doms, and the women are masochistic subs. Most of them get off on being passed around."

"It sounds worse than it is," said Ella, jumping in.

"Anyway, that's what happens there," Juliet said. "And Milo's into that, but he's pretty sure you wouldn't be. It stresses him out a lot."

"Do you still go? With Fort?" I stared in disbelief at her engagement ring.

"Sometimes we go, and sometimes he invites other people into our scenes, men and women. We have to be in a certain mood, but it can be exciting. You don't think so, though," she said, reading my face. "And Milo's aware of that. He told Fort he didn't want to get into a deeper relationship with you for fear you'd get freaked out at all his perversions."

"What are the other rules?" Now that I'd heard a couple of them, I needed to know them all. I needed to know what I was dealing with here, when it came to Milo's "perversions."

"Let's see," said Ella. "Rule three, no safe words allowed."

"No safe words? That's not acceptable. It's not safe, sane, and consensual if you can't end a scene."

"It's kind of a fetish thing," said Juliet. "And it's acceptable to people who are into playing that way. It's called consensual non-consent."

"But..." I'd never heard of this consensual non-consent thing in my research. "If they're doing real BDSM, they have to use safe words, right?"

"What's real BDSM, though?" asked Juliet. "Every woman who goes to the club signs a form at the door agreeing to the rules, including the non-use of safe words. As long as everyone gets off on it, it's okay."

I wanted to argue, but I felt my lack of experience while I searched for the right words. Could she be right? I didn't know. I was a beginner. I had no idea things like "no safe words" could even go on. "What else?" I asked.

"There's a uniform," said Juliet. "Rule four is that all the women have to wear it."

"Your tits and ass hang out." Ella grinned. "But it is pretty flattering in a harness-corset kind of way."

"I like the stockings."

"Oh, yes," said Ella. "And the collar."

"You have to wear a collar?" I asked.

"All women wear the same uniform and collar, in order to show their submission to the men. And the last rule is just that you have to follow the other rules, or you aren't allowed to play there. The whole thing is very gothic-pervert, but when you're in the club and everyone's scening together, you get turned on. You can't help it."

"Well..." Juliet regarded me with sympathy. "Most people get turned on."

I didn't know what to think. I remembered Milo's pained expression when I'd talked about Underworld, thinking I was so "in the know." He must have been trying not to laugh.

"This is a lot to take in," I said, as the silence lengthened. "But thank you for telling me. I understand now why he felt like...like I might not get into that side of him."

"He didn't want to hurt you," Juliet said. "He kept repeating that to Fort, that he wanted you so much, but he didn't want to hurt you. He wants to preserve the friendship you've had all these years. He told Fort it was 'so pure.' He wants to keep being your friend, Alice. That's why he regrets things going as far as they did."

It's too dangerous. I'm afraid you don't really understand the sexual sadism thing. That's what he'd told me after he took me to his dungeon, tormented me, fucked me in the ass.

"What are..." I swallowed hard, not knowing how to ask. "What are the worst things he likes to do there? Like, the most extreme stuff?"

Ella and Juliet exchanged a glance, and Ella said, "Oh, Alice, it's nothing criminal. It's not extreme in a BDSM sense. He's not killing women or anything."

It didn't reassure me that "he's not killing women" was their initial qualifier. "What is he doing to women, then?" I asked.

"He's a sadist, a hardcore sadist," said Juliet. "Like, not in a cute, slap and tickle, sugar-coated kind of way. He's not into fur paddles and pink ball gags. He likes to get a pain reaction, and make his partners cry. He likes to gang up on women who are already being dominated, so they'll hurt worse. He uses whips, clamps, uncomfortable bondage. He slaps women and chokes them."

"He slapped me so many times once that Devin beat him up," added Ella. "I mean, I was enjoying it." A flush rose beneath her neck and cheeks. "I'm sorry, I'm making things worse."

"Definitely," said Juliet.

"No, it's okay." *Just wait a minute, while I try to process the image of Milo slapping you hard enough to anger your boyfriend, and you liking it.*

"He wasn't hitting me that hard. It was kinky fun, but Devin has issues around abuse."

Juliet broke in. "Everyone has issues around abuse at The Gallery, because that's not what BDSM is about."

"Now you said the name of it." Ella shook a finger at her friend, then turned to me. "Please forget you heard that."

"Excuse me for being shaken up that you would tell Alice about that whole debacle with Dev." Juliet covered her eyes, then took a breath. "Believe me, it wasn't abusive slapping, and that's not the only thing Milo does there, go around slapping women across the face."

"And when he played with the two of us, that's all it was—play. There was no emotional attachment. It was just kinky stuff, because I was with Devin, and Juliet has been in love with Fort since way before she met Milo."

"So he's played with both of you?"

Now Juliet was blushing too. "Yeah. A handful of times. Literally, I can count on one hand the number of times."

"We don't really like to play with him, because he's so..." Ella paused. "So hard to play with. He's not afraid to leave bruises, or, you know, make you gag and cry. But he only plays as hard as you can take. He never did anything to Juliet or me that was too much. When he wants to do really extreme stuff, he plays with women who enjoy that kind of scening."

"Right," Juliet agreed. "The Dominants at The Gallery have a code they follow too, their own set of rules they self-enforce. To be members, they have to agree not to take more than any sub is willing to give, and to never, ever fuck with the vulnerable. That's a big one, to only bring women to The Gallery who can handle it." She paused, probably thinking that I was iffy in that regard. "Milo's always been really careful about picking partners. He ends up with the wildest subs because they want a Dom with his intensity. It's always consensual, even if the club's a 'no safe word' environment. He's so conscientious, Alice, so particular about only playing with women who can handle him."

Women who can handle him. In other words, women who weren't me. *I'm not rejecting you*, he'd told me. *I'm trying to protect you.* We didn't have a future because he thought I'd never be able to enjoy the things he was into.

"I'm glad you came here to talk to me about this," I said, close to tears. "It was hard to hear, but at least I understand now. He didn't tell me any of this, he just said we wouldn't work out."

"Do you love him?" asked Juliet.

121

I blinked at her. "Of course I do. I suppose I always will, on some existential level. Does that matter now?"

"I'm only asking because I wasn't that hardcore when I met Fort. I mean, I never would have considered going to a place with those crazy rules, but I fell for him so hard that I gave it a try, and I ended up being more into it than I expected."

"That's true," said Ella. "You might never be into the edgiest stuff he likes, but if you go up the kink ladder to meet him, maybe he can come down to meet you, and you can connect somewhere in the middle."

I frowned. "Not sure I want him to have to go backwards for me."

"He would, though," said Juliet. "I heard him talking to Fort. I heard the pain in his voice." She touched me with her sparkling-ring hand. "No love is perfect, you know? There are always compromises. Milo's rarely the compromising type, but I'm sure he'd do it for you."

Ella let out a soft sigh. "Well, we've given you a lot to think about. We'll get out of your hair, but if you need anything, or if you have any problems with the apartment, you have my number."

"Thanks."

We all stood, me and the two other women Milo had "scened" with. I thanked them again at the door, for their candor, and for their clarification of Milo's issues. I understood now why he'd never confide the extent of his BDSM life to me. Because yes, I would have tried anything to win his heart. I would have put on the sexy uniform and collar and given myself to other men if that's what he required to make things work. I might not have liked it, but I would have done it. He wasn't only protecting me from him, when he shot down our continuing relationship.

He was protecting me from myself.

Chapter Thirteen: Milo

I was working late when my phone rang, flashing Fort's name. I put down the delicate body of Alice's violin, only recently assembled and glued. "What's up?" I asked.

"Hey, Milo. Are you on speaker?"

"No."

"So..." He paused. I could hear a soft female whine over the connection. "I have a bad little subbie here beside me, confessing that she tried to make things better between you and Alice, and may have ended up making things worse."

I imagined him twisting her nipple, drawing out those whining cries. "You'd better start at the beginning," I said.

"I guess Juliet overheard some of our conversation the other night."

Fuck. The conversation we'd had over two bottles of wine, while I was feeling emo as shit?

"She knows she's not supposed to eavesdrop." He paused as the whine rose to a cry. "But she was worried about you, and she thought if she spoke to Alice, she could help her understand...what was it you said, darling?"

"Help her understand about Milo," said a soft voice.

"What about Milo?"

I didn't hear anything else for a moment, only crying. "Fort, don't torment her," I said. "I'm sure she meant well."

"Maybe, but I beat her little tail anyway. She and Ella paid a visit to Alice to tell her the reason you were resisting a relationship, and I'm afraid they told her too much."

"Too much?" I asked.

"Too much. Everything. You. Me. Them. Your kinks. The Gallery."

I sucked in a breath. "They told Alice about The Gallery?"

"She said they didn't mean to, but the name slipped out. They were in the process of telling her the rules—"

"Fuck. That's not okay."

"I know, I know. If you want, you can come over and punish her too."

I was tempted. The Gallery's members were sworn to discretion. But I doubted there was much left of her "little tail" to punish, judging by her whimpers in the background. "I don't want to punish her any more, but I need to speak to her. Will you put her on the phone?"

"Sure."

"I'm sorry, Milo," she wailed a moment later. I held the phone a little farther from my ear as she apologized two more times. "We didn't mean to say so much to Alice. It just came out. We were trying to help her understand you better."

"It sounds like you did a bang up job of that." I softened the edge in my voice. "I know you were trying to help, but I didn't want her to know those things about me."

"She didn't react badly. Well, I mean, she was surprised." Juliet sniffled. "It was a lot for her to take in."

"You must have known it would be," I scolded. "And it was my private business. My choice whether to tell her or not."

"I know. We only wanted to help. When we got there, Ella and I could tell she's been feeling sad without you. Her eyes had that look, you know?"

Her words stabbed into my heart. Yes, I knew that look. I remembered it from the days after the Michelin building caught fire, and she lost everything.

"So...what did she say?" I wanted to know, even though I dreaded knowing. "Did she look scared? Disgusted?"

Juliet's pause told me everything I needed to know. "I think it was just a shock, Milo. And then Ella spilled about the time you were slapping her, and Dev beat you up, and it came out that you'd played with the two of us, also."

"Ah," I said, anger flaring along my nerves. "So you told her absolutely everything. I might come punish you after all."

"You can if you want," she said, breaking up in sobs. "I deserve it, but maybe wait until tomorrow."

I heard a yelp, probably Fort pinching one of the welts he'd deposited on her ass, to make her cry so hard.

"If he wants to punish you, he can do it anytime," Fort said sternly.

"Tell your Sir to give you some corner time with clamps on," I said, "while you think about discretion and privacy. Put him back on the phone."

She apologized once more and handed it over. While I waited for Fort to come back on, I thought of ways I might put a positive spin on what had happened. I couldn't think of one.

"I'm back," he said. "And she's in the corner. She's really sorry, Milo."

"At least she told you what she did. Otherwise, I wouldn't know that Alice knows."

"Jules meant well, but Jesus, she rarely fucks up this bad. We haven't had a punishment session in a while. I'm sure Ella's also feeling Devin's wrath right about now."

"Which she deserves."

He chuckled at my irritated response. "Look, this is life, man. Try not to be too torn up about it all."

I thought a moment before I spoke. "I would have preferred to keep that part of my life away from her, but if she knows, she knows. At least she understands now. I guess that's what Juliet and Ella were aiming for. Anyway, I'd better go." I looked down at the violin I was making for Alice. "Give your naughty sub a hug when she's done with her corner time. Tell her I forgive her."

"Will do. Talk to you soon."

We hung up, and I was left with silence and spiraling thoughts. Would it have been better to tell her on my own, rather than having her learn about The Gallery from someone else? Too late to do anything about that now.

I'd have to see Alice soon, to make final adjustments to her violin before I assembled it for good. Stronger glue, more varnish, and tighter strings so she could make any tone she wanted. I traced the small heart I'd hidden in this instrument's wood grain. Still in the same place on the back, but less obvious this time, because I was better at hiding things than I'd been when I was a younger man.

Maybe I could catch her after one of her Met Orchestra concerts, and make her play a few notes so I could see how my earlier measurements had fared. I wasn't looking forward to the awkwardness, but I still loved her, and I was making her a violin with my heart on it and in it, whether she wanted the damn thing or not.

* * * * *

I bought a ticket to her Met concert the following night, and worked myself up all day to see her. So she knew about me and The Gallery, and whatever else Jules and Ella had told her in some effort to "fix things" between us. Okay. There was no way to go back.

But we were still longtime friends, and fellow musicians. My mind wandered as I watched her play. I tried to read the set of her shoulders and the way she pursed her lips. Her hair looked braided to the point of painful tightness, and she wasn't happy with the violin she was playing. I could tell by the way she overplayed notes that ought to have been light and carefree. They were doing Mozart tonight. Poor thing.

After the show, it was easy to get backstage. The Fierro name counted for a lot in the music world, especially when I was carrying a violin case under my arm. I asked around until I found Alice in a mostly deserted corridor, chatting with a couple other violinists. One of the two men wanted to sleep with her, or had already slept with her, based on his body language. I gritted my teeth and leaned against the wall where she would see me and the violin case. I didn't want to join her conversation, but I also wouldn't let her leave without talking to me. When she tried to slip away, pretending not to see me, I called out her name.

"Lilly-Alice!"

Then I wondered why I'd used her full name. To show her I meant business? To remind her that I'd known her during her Lala years?

"Hi," she said, turning to me. "What are you doing here?"

"I came to watch you play."

She couldn't hold my gaze. "I didn't think you liked Mozart."

"I don't. Not my favorite. But I wanted to see you, and I wanted to bring you this."

She stared at the violin case like I was holding out a tarantula.

"It's assembled and stringed," I said. "I'd like you to play it so I can see if any adjustments need to be made."

She cast an annoyed look around the corridor, then led me into one of the soundproof warmup rooms behind the stage. The room wasn't that big, so we were suddenly alone, and close.

"I told you, you didn't have to do this." She took the case, but didn't open it.

"I did have to do it. By the way, the instrument you're playing now is a piece of shit. You didn't buy that, did you?"

"I'm borrowing it," she said through tight lips.

"Good. Give it back. I'll have the Pressenda delivered to your apartment tomorrow."

"Stop." Her voice was sharp, even if she looked at the floor instead of me. "Stop trying to shove your kindness shit in my face."

"This isn't 'kindness shit,'" I said, my own temper sparking. "This is a nice fucking violin that I spent many hours making for you, because you deserve to have the best fucking violin in the world. Now I need you to play it for me, so I can finish the goddamned thing."

Her stubborn features crumpled, and she burst into tears, hugging the case against her chest. "I miss you," she said.

"I miss you too. Come here."

I took her in my arms, the violin case wedged between us.

"I don't mean to be a bitch," she murmured against my shoulder. "I don't know why I'm angry with you. I mean, I know why, but I still love you. I can't believe you still made me a violin."

"I told you I would."

She drew away from me. I held the case while she wiped at tears, then she sat in one of the two chairs in the small room. I sat in the other and took out the instrument I'd built for her.

"It's only partially glued, so it's delicate," I said, handing it to her. "You don't need to play that much. Just enough for me to see the way..." *The way to finish it.* Were we finished, Lala Nyquist and I? There was a new and uneasy tension between us. It would probably always be there, because I hadn't had the strength to keep my dick in my pants.

"This is so pretty, Milo." She ran a finger along the edge of the fingerboard, and around the curve of the lower bout. "It's so beautiful." She gazed at the trim I'd placed along the center of the scroll and plucked one of the strings. I could see her tumbling into love with it, and it made everything that came before this moment worthwhile.

"I used those strings you like," I said. "The heavy-gauge gut. They'll take a while to stretch, but they'll suit this instrument's tone."

"You thought of everything."

She was still gazing at it, like a mother at her newborn child. I nudged her knee with mine. "Play it, Alice. Let's hear how it sounds."

She looked teary again, but she collected herself and lifted the violin to her shoulder, positioning it beneath her chin. I watched to be sure it fit comfortably, that my measurements had been accurate. She settled right into it. "Nice," she said. "Hand me my bow?"

I gave her the bow she'd used for tonight's performance. I imagined she *had* bought that, because it suited her tone and playing style far better than the violin she'd borrowed. She closed her eyes before she drew it across the strings in an open A.

"It might need a little tuning," I said.

"It's fine."

She played a few more notes, gently turning the pegs and using the tuners to get the tone she wanted. I watched her expression as she played a short violin piece by her favorite composer, Vivaldi. The fit was true, and the sound she produced lifted the hair on my arms. It was that amazing. This new instrument was as good as the Grapeleaf, or better, and it wasn't even finished yet.

"Oh, Milo," she said when she lifted the bow.

She was in love with the violin. I couldn't give her everything she wanted from me, but I could give her this. She touched my hand, like words were beyond her. "How did you do this?" she finally asked. "It's perfect."

"Because I know you. I know what you need."

I meant the words in reference to the instrument, but in the small room, with the emotions flowing, they sounded dangerously sexual. She turned the instrument over in her lap, trying to hide the blush that her Nordic skin always gave away. Then her eyes widened.

"Oh, wow."

"What?"

She touched the back, traced her fingers over the small heart I thought I'd hidden so well in the maple and varnish. "There was a heart shape like this in the grain of my old violin. That's kind of amazing, to have it happen twice." She looked up at me then. My face must have given me away. "You did this? You made the heart?"

"Yes."

"To make it look like my old one?"

I laughed, a rueful, self-conscious sound. "I had a small hand in making your Grapeleaf, Alice. When I was alone in the studio with it, applying varnish, I hid a heart on it too. My father never knew." I paused, thinking of the many times he and my mother had pushed me toward Alice. "Or maybe he did. Anyway, it shouldn't affect the tone."

She blinked down at the heart. "Why didn't you tell me you put a heart on the Grapeleaf? Why didn't you show me? It would have made it more special to me."

I laughed again. "You were in love with some other boy then, some adolescent Swedish beefcake. I couldn't compete." I'd been skinny and pimply well into my twenties, and always so dark against her joy and lightness. Her perfection.

She shook her head. "I wasn't in love with that guy. Puppy love, maybe, but only because you were out of reach." She traced the back of the violin, noting all the care I'd taken to create smooth, solid resonance in the fluid lines. "Thank you for this. For everything."

"I hope it brings you a lot of money when you sell it. I'll have it done in a couple weeks, if you want to line up some buyers."

She gave a half-tearful laugh. "You know I'm not selling it. I'm going to have to find an apartment with a fire and explosion proof chamber built in, because if I ever lost this thing, it would kill me."

She handed back the violin, and I put it in the case I'd also fashioned especially for her, or, at least, her instrument. She put away her bow and we stood to move toward the door, but we bumped into each other in the cramped space. I reached to steady her, smiling. She gazed back at me, not quite smiling.

I wasn't sure what happened then. A spark, a need, a re-ignition of the pull we couldn't shake. I cupped her face between my hands, pressing my fingertips to the lattice of her braids as our lips connected. *Be gentle. Show her you're not the monster she's heard about.* But I was that monster, and she shredded my control.

She whimpered at my violent kiss, and gave it back in kind. I was still holding the violin, she was still clutching her bow. The shit violin she'd played earlier was somewhere at our feet, so I couldn't shove her to the ground and rip off her clothes even if I wanted to. We were in a soundproof room, and I wanted to make her scream, but this wasn't the time or place.

"We need to talk," I said, nudging her away.

"No. Talking won't change anything." She pulled me close again, staring in my eyes. "We need to take the leap and be done with it. Enough is enough."

CHAPTER FOURTEEN: ALICE

Blue yipped with pleasure when Milo escorted me into his living room, but neither of us stopped to pet him. We stashed the instruments on the kitchen counter, out of the reach of a certain dog's curious, wet nose.

"Bedroom or dungeon?" Milo asked.

That was a stupid question. The dungeon was the place he could be himself, and the place our sparks really flew. "Take me to your dungeon, and show me more things," I told him.

He hustled me down the hall. "Do you remember the safe word?"

"I've been dreaming about it," I said, which was the truth.

We went inside and he flicked on the lights, more than he'd put on the first time. We undressed, shedding our clothes, eager to get naked together. I'd wanted to see him again for so long, unable to get the image of his nude glory out of my mind. The olive-toned muscles. The broad shoulders. The already-hard cock. It was then, as I stared at his huge, hard shaft, that I remembered there would be pain to pay to get what I wanted.

I looked around the dungeon, seeing it with new eyes. I thought he'd played hard with me before, but it had been, apparently, just a taste of what he was into. Would I survive this next encounter? I hoped so, because I wanted more. More of him, more of his urges, more of his hot, wicked perversions.

"Milo," I said, holding out a hand when he tried to kiss me again. "I want you to know that I—I want to try—I want to try what you like, but I'm not only doing it for you. I've fantasized about the things we've done together. I've masturbated to the memories so many times."

He gazed at me. "You have?"

"Yes, so please, don't worry that you have to hold back. I have the safe word if I need it, and I trust you."

"It's not that easy, to just *trust me*." He fisted his cock. "What if you hate something I do to you? What if it makes you hate me?"

"Then I'll safe word my way out of things. But I really think I'll enjoy whatever you do." I wanted to pinch my own nipples, hurt my own breasts, out of anticipation. I wanted to squeeze my own pussy, which was already dripping wet, just from the intent look on his face. "Please, Milo. Let's try."

He came at me so fast, I didn't have time to step back before he took my face between his hands. "I love you so much, Alice. What is it about you? Why are my feelings for you so strong, so fucking voracious that I hate myself?"

"Don't hate yourself." I gazed at him in entreaty. "Tie me up. Hurt me."

He made a feral-sounding growl in his throat and led me to the X-shaped St. Andrew's Cross. He put my back against the slightly angled structure, and I stared at him as he bound my arms above my head, one wrist to each crosspiece, and then bound my elbows as well. The position forced my breasts out, bringing a delicious feeling of vulnerability. My legs were bound next, first at the ankle and then just above my knees.

I could wiggle—a little—but I couldn't escape, no matter how I moved my hands or danced on my toes. Milo watched me, a glint of satisfaction in his gaze. *He loves when you struggle*, I thought. *He loves that you can't get away.*

"How does that feel?" he asked.

"Wonderful. And scary."

He lifted one of his dark brows. "Good. Now, less wonderful, and more scary." His eyes were dark too, on fire. "Since you're willing, we're going to try some new, interesting things. A few more painful things."

"Yes, Sir."

"We'll see if you like them. Well, if you can take them without safe wording."

My voice quavered. "O-okay."

He went to his row of storage cabinets, opened a long drawer, and took out a clear Lucite rod. It was thin, even bendy. Almost pretty. He returned to the front of me and tapped it against one of my nipples.

I yelped. God, it stung. He tapped the other and I started flailing around. "Too much?" he asked.

It kind of was, but I shook my head because I wanted to challenge myself. I wanted to get to the magical place where the pain started to feel good. He laughed and put down the Lucite tool, and went for a small, braided leather whip. It didn't look any friendlier, and when he flicked it against my stomach, I let out another cry of alarm at the hot pain. "How does that feel?" he asked.

"It...it stings, Sir."

"Stand still for it," he said, but I couldn't. I danced on my toes, twisting my torso as far as I could while he flicked each of my breasts.

"You're not being very still." He was enjoying this, lecturing me, frightening me. I wondered what else was in those drawers. "I think I have a solution for your problem."

He crossed in my line of sight to another cabinet of scariness. When he opened the door, I got an eyeful of metal dildos and anal plugs in graduating sizes. At first, I thought he intended to plug me, but he brought a dildo instead, thick and hard, about eight inches long, wider at the bottom and tapering toward the top. Not quite as big as his cock, but almost.

"What is that for?"

"Hush."

He was rubbing it with lubricant, and I saw that the base had a small, flat flange. "Hips forward," he said, making me arch them away from the cross as much as my bonds would let me. As soon as I did so, he attached the dildo to the cross with a metallic click.

I knew by now what was happening, how he intended to stop me from squirming around. "I'll try harder to be still, Sir," I began, as he nudged my hips back. My asshole stretched around the solid metal tip.

"You know what to do," he said, ignoring my words. "Sink back on it. It's well lubricated."

"I can be still on my own. I promise I'll be more still from now on."

"Yes, you will, with this in your ass."

Oww... My legs tensed as I eased back onto the dildo. It wasn't unbearable pain, but it was uncomfortable and humiliating. He lifted my chin, forcing me to look in his dark brown eyes as I bit my lip and whimpered. How stern he could look, and how sexy it made him. It made the pain a tiny bit easier to bear.

"Good enough," he said. "That'll keep you where you're supposed to be."

Between the shaft in my ass and the bonds around my arms and legs, I felt dangerously controlled—and aroused. I'd been able to move a little before; now any movement made the shaft slide in my asshole, creating a clit-aching feeling of sexual slavery. Oh God, I wanted sex. I wanted to be fucked, and not just by a metal dildo. I stared at his hard, bobbing cock, wondering how long he'd make me wait.

135

He turned away and went for something else to torment me with. I closed my eyes, afraid to look. When he pinched my nipples, my worst fears were realized. He held a pair of wicked looking black clamps.

"If you want to be with me, Alice, you have to get used to these." He dangled them in front of my eyes. "I use them almost every time, because it's a really fast way to make you hurt. These are going to hurt more than the last ones, okay?"

"Yes, Sir."

His quiet warning did nothing to prepare me for the burst of torment when he applied the first clamp. They weren't just strong, they were heavy. I gasped, struggling against the pain, getting fucked by the dildo in my ass because I couldn't keep still. I tried to twist away from the other clamp, but of course, that was impossible. He gave me a sympathetic look that was nonetheless pleased. "I know, they're awful," he said. "They're called clover clamps, and they come in bigger sizes, for the record. I won't leave them on longer than ten minutes or so."

Ten minutes? I needed them off now. I could have safe worded. It would have ended the pain of the nipple clamps, at least, but just as I thought of the word *Lala*, something kicked on in my brain, something that had me clenching my asshole and pussy, hovering on the edge of an orgasm. I exhaled in short, jerky bursts, caught between terror and a horrid kind of ecstasy.

Then the whip was back, flicking my upper thighs, my hips and stomach, my breasts, making any chance at an orgasm disappear. I cried out at each blow, then sobbed a plea as they grew progressively harder. He ignored me, because I wasn't supposed to beg for mercy. His only reaction was a concentrated smile. I fucked myself on the dildo as a kind of soothing mechanism, because it hurt less than being whipped. The indignity of it made tears well in my eyes.

When he stopped, I sagged against the cross, as much as the dildo would let me. "I know," he said, placing the whip beneath my chin to tilt my head up for another kiss. "It hurts, doesn't it? But you're feeling pleasure too." As he said this, he slid his hand down and parted my pussy lips. I was so wet, so sopping *drenched*, that I felt humiliated anew. "Maybe this thing between us, Alice..." he said, his lips against my temple. "Maybe we have a chance."

I nodded, because I couldn't speak. Every time I moved, the clamps swung, making me tremble at the renewed pain. I felt stinging, hot lines all over my body from the whip. He hadn't been as gentle as last time, I guess because I wasn't a beginner anymore. I'd finally calmed myself down when he put down the whip and picked up the Lucite implement again.

"I won't hurt you," he said, tracing over some of the hot spots he'd already left. "Not that badly."

He didn't hit me with the Lucite rod at first. Instead, he slid it along my stomach and down between my pussy lips. It glazed over my clit, slick and hard, and I arched my hips, straining to feel it again, fighting against the shaft in my ass.

"Oh, you like that?" he murmured. "Feels good?"

I made a garbled noise of assent.

"You're such a maso. But I should have known."

He drew the rod back and smacked my clit with it, a sharp explosion of pain. "Oh God," I whispered. "Oh God, Oh God."

"God's not listening right now. Only me." He slid it along my clit again, and the feelings of pleasure warred with dread of the flick that would surely follow. Even so, I couldn't help grinding against it. The clamps swung from my nipples, with biting, dull pain.

"What a good girl you're being," he said. "Let's take a break for a minute. Let your hair down."

His fingers ran along my scalp, separating my painstakingly neat braids into loose tendrils that tickled my temples and cheeks. It was a soft, gentle feeling, in contrast to the other pain he was visiting on me. Every few strands, he stopped and kissed me, sometimes softly, sometimes with violent passion or a frightening bite.

"Are you ready for more?" he asked, when all my braids were unraveled.

"My nipples hurt, Sir. They hurt a lot."

"I know." He brought the rod up with a crisp *thwack* between my pussy lips, then flicked the bare skin above my mons as I bobbed on my toes. "Ow, ow, ow."

"This isn't anything yet. Just beginner stuff."

Maybe so, but my ass hurt, my thighs hurt, my nipples were killing me, and my pussy was on fire with both lust and searing pain. I stared at him, not knowing how to express all the things I was feeling, not knowing what to say. His eyes held mine, a comfort from the storm within me.

"Are you going to cry for me, baby?"

"I don't know." But I was already crying. As the rod flicked me again, a tear rolled down my cheek. It hurt *so bad*. I wanted him *so much*. He started to stroke me again, drawing the smooth Lucite over my center like a bow on violin strings. The punishment came after, always. First the pleasure, then the flick of his wrist, and agony in my most tender, sexual center. More tears flowed. I made no effort to hold them back, because I knew he wanted me to cry. There was something freeing about letting the emotion out, and I could tell he loved it. He put his hand on my neck and stared down at my damp cheeks, kissing away a few tears.

"Do you need me to stop, Alice?"

"No," I said, as his fingers stroked my exposed throat. "I like it. Mostly. It's just scary, a little."

"Sometimes it's fun to be scared. Sometimes being scared turns people on." He put down the rod, caressing my sore pussy flesh. I could feel the afterburn of every stroke he'd landed, pulsing in a hot line. Why did that turn me on so much? Why was I crying at the same time?

He drove his fingers deep inside my pussy, so deep I could barely contain them, with the dildo still stretching my ass. With his other hand, he took off the clamps. Only his fingers—and the dildo—kept me in place as sensation stormed back to my nipples. I took shallow, halting breaths, and more tears overflowed. As he held my gaze, I realized I'd never felt so vulnerable, so endangered, as I did in that moment. I'd had sex so many times, plenty of times, and I'd always felt in control, calm, satisfied. This kind of sex had nothing to do with that.

Because this wasn't just sex, it was possession. His fingers probed and controlled me, asserting his dominance, telling me everything I needed to know. He pinched my sore, sensitive nipples and I tried to jerk away. Then he slapped my face, and...

And...

And I liked it. I got even more turned on.

Ella had told me she liked it, and I couldn't believe she meant it, but now I understood. My pussy pulsed around his fingers. He gave a small, wicked smile, and I thought he might slap me again, but he only kissed me, harder than any of the times he'd kissed me yet. He ended up with his fingers wrapped around my neck again, and I could hardly bear how excited that made me feel.

"Please, Sir. Don't let me go."

I kept repeating that, *Don't let me go*, swallowing against the pressure of his palm. I wanted him to help me come. I wanted him to fuck me, because I wanted to come with him inside me, possessing me.

"I don't think I can fit inside your hot little pussy with that dildo in your ass. Come here, baby."

He undid the bonds and eased me off the cross. I fell to my knees, partly because my legs wouldn't hold me, and partly because it seemed like the proper place for me to be in this dungeon. He lifted me and carried me to the bondage bed against the back wall, and pushed me onto it, positioning me on my hands and knees. He made me wait there as he rolled on a rubber. No bondage, but I didn't care. I was dying to be touched. To be fucked.

He used his fingers to fuck my pussy again, pressing them deep, just grazing over my clit so I went wild but got no release. I thought I'd die from wanting him inside me. "Crawl," he ordered, slapping my ass. "Crawl to the headboard and reach for the highest bar."

I obeyed, stretching my arms as high as I could, desperate to please him. He was behind me in an instant, pinning me against the metal lattice, grabbing my hips and impaling me as I clung to the bar above me. I arched my back, trying to hold on, but it felt so good my fingers loosened. His hands came over mine, gripping them so I couldn't let go. I could feel his heat behind me, and oh, the way his cock filled me...

"It...feels...so...good," I said as he pounded me. My knees were spread on the white sheets, and I bucked against the air, wishing I could rub myself to an instant orgasm. No, that would be too quick. I wanted to revel in his rough lovemaking until my body couldn't take it anymore.

"Let go," he said. "Turn around towards me."

I let go of the bar and changed position. Once again, he made me lift my hands and hang on, but now we were facing each other. He grasped my hips and drove into me from his knees, forcing my pussy onto his cock. Our chests collided in time to his thrusts, his scent and ragged breaths driving my arousal to its highest peak. My ass felt empty now, but my pussy was so, so full of him. He banged me there against his headboard, and it hurt, but it felt magical too, and when he started grinding his pelvis against my clit, I lost it.

"I can't— Oh God. I'm going to come."

He wrapped his arms around me, holding me as our bodies smacked together. He was so encompassing, so deep inside me, and around me at the same time. When my orgasm exploded, I lost my grip on the bed, but he caught me so I didn't fall. He held me. Protected me. I let go of the headboard and wrapped myself around him, burying my face against his hair. He pushed in me once more, until I could feel him pulsing inside me. His groan was louder than my breathless orgasm whimpers.

Without speaking, without leaving me, he pulled us backward, holding my hips so I was sprawled on top of him on the bed. I squeezed involuntarily on his cock, aftershocks from my powerful orgasm. "Holy

Christ," he said, and reached down to pull out of me. While I lay back on the bed, he took care of the condom, then returned and crawled over my sprawled body.

"I think I'm dead now," I said.

He stroked my hair. "Not dead. Just tired."

I gazed up at him, wondering how I could feel shy after all we'd just done together. "We went a little harder that time."

"Yes." His fingers stopped in my hair, then started up again. "I'm glad you said 'we.' I don't want this to just be about me. I mean, I don't want you to do things you don't like because I..." His voice trailed off.

I laughed softly. "I'm pretty sure I liked everything you did to me, even the painful stuff I didn't like. I think those things turned me on most of all."

"Alice..." He studied me for a long, silent moment. "You're not just saying that because you want us to work, are you?"

"No. I'm not. Do you think I'd lie to you?"

"It's important. Lala. Alice. Listen." He cradled my face in his hands. "It's important to me that you don't settle for something in this relationship that's not your absolute ideal. That wouldn't be okay."

"Do you think I can fake the things my body did? They were real reactions." I was getting kind of upset. This wasn't the type of pillow talk I wanted.

"Shh. Okay. I believe you. But if we...if we do this thing...this relationship...you're going to have to get used to me checking in. Not for you, but for me. You know I don't..." He ducked his head and pressed his lips to my cheek. "I don't want to hurt you. Not in a bad way."

I turned my face so he would kiss my lips. I didn't like seeing him so worried, and I tried to express all the willingness and tenderness I felt as we ran our hands over each other's bodies. When we parted with a sigh, I threw my arms around him.

"I'm so happy. We should be happy, Milo. We *are* kind of compatible."

"Kind of?" He smiled, and I hoped—oh God, I hoped—everything would be okay. "We're compatible, yes. I'm starting to believe that, but we have to keep the lines of communication open. You're still a mostly-beginner. Yes, even with all the things I've done to you," he added, heading off my protest.

"I'd hate to see what I have to go through to not be a beginner anymore." I pouted, then brightened. "I guess we'll just have to keep doing more kinky scenes."

"That should be easy. Seems to happen with the two of us whether we want it or not."

"And that club you like, the one Juliet and Ella told me about? Maybe we could work up to that too."

He studied me, perhaps considering my worthiness to be invited into that secret enclave. "Maybe. The Gallery would be a big step."

"After The Gallery, I wouldn't be a beginner anymore, would I?"

He narrowed his eyes, giving me what I had come to think of as his "Dominant" look. "This is hard for me, you know."

"What is?"

"Being rough with you. Putting marks on you and bringing you deeper into the lifestyle." He parted my thighs, tracing the lingering red marks the Lucite rod had left on my pussy lips. "It's hard bringing you down from your pedestal to hurt you."

"I was never on a pedestal, unless you put me there."

"We come to the crux of the problem. I put you up there a long time ago. This is going to take some time for me, Alice."

"That's fine." I said it quickly. I didn't want him to think too much about why he shouldn't hurt me. I just wanted him to hurt me again. "We can take as long as you like. Just know that I loved tonight, and I'd love to go with you to The Gallery, when you think I'm ready for it. If you wanted me to go."

"What if I take you to The Gallery and you find another Dominant you like more than me?"

He said it in a jokey way, but there was some deeper emotion. Possessiveness? Jealousy? Surely he knew I'd never love anyone more than him. No one else could give me the history, the kindness, the talent, the connection running through our veins. I didn't care about playing with other men, except that it might excite him, and deepen our power-exchange bonds.

"Stay here tonight?" he asked, changing the subject.

"Yes, Sir. That would be great."

"And move back in tomorrow? Blue would love it."

"And you?" I asked, laughing.

"I'd love it more. I'd carry your shit here myself from Lower Manhattan. Carry it on my fucking back like a pack mule."

He kissed me then, but with some wistfulness, some reserve beneath the love and warmth. I knew some part of him was still afraid he'd hurt me by accident. And what if things didn't work out? What would we do? How could we overcome that?

I huddled against him, pushing those possibilities away. I loved him more than I thought I'd ever love anyone. We were bound by fate to make this relationship work.

CHAPTER FIFTEEN: MILO

I walked into Coleman's Steakhouse fifteen minutes late, after dropping off Alice at Lincoln Center. She'd been late for her call time, too. Since we'd moved ahead with our relationship, things had gotten crazy in my Bridgeport apartment. Now that my resistance had crumbled, we were making up for lost time, for years of unrequited longing. My dungeon had never seen so much action. As I crossed to my friends' table, I could still taste the faint hint of her on my lips.

"He appears," said Fort, raising a glass. "Out from the clutches of his draining love affair."

"Here's to getting drained," Dev chimed in, taking a drink. "We got some Lobster Cocktail for starters, Milo."

They both chuckled at the word "cocktail" like a couple of eleven-year-old boys. They were enjoying the fact that I'd been sucked into my own love affair, after all my scoffing and insistence that relationships weren't for me. I was enjoying being in love, more than I ever hoped I would. Over the past few weeks, Alice and I had grown close to the point of pain. Well, her pain, my pleasure.

"Glad you could make it out," Fort said as I sat across from them.

"Sorry I'm late. I had to drop Alice at the theater." *After I finished whipping her ass and fucking her, which took a delightfully long time.* Once she got me going, I forgot everything else—her work, my work, even dinner reservations made weeks in advance. I gave myself a moment to imagine my masochistic lover shifting on her sore cheeks under the gaze of the audience and conductor at tonight's concert. For two weeks now, she'd had some kind of marks on her ass, because I couldn't resist her. I was finally coming to terms with her insistence that it was okay. "What are you guys drinking?" I asked.

"A Santa Maria Pinot Noir," said Dev. "Have some. It's good for your heart."

I accepted a glass and took a sip, the wine blending deliciously with Alice's lingering scent. I must have had that "look," because both of them smiled at me.

"So, things still going well?" asked Fort.

"Yeah, very well." I tried not to look too smug. "Very, very well."

"How's the violin coming?"

"Almost finished. Just a week or so left for the glue to cure, and she can take it to the Met with her. But my mother has to think of a name for the violin first."

"Your mother?" asked Dev. "Why your mother?"

"Because his grandmother died," said Fort. "Remember? She used to name them. Now his mother names them."

Yes, and Alice will name them one day. The thought came to me so naturally, so clearly, that I almost said it out loud. I already pictured Alice as my future wife, a dangerous assumption when our romantic relationship was still relatively new. I took a deep drink of wine, glad that my olive Italian skin didn't show a blush.

145

"So, my mom's thinking over names," I said. "Alice and I have a vote too. She already vetoed the name 'Lala.'"

Dev grinned. "The Lala? That wouldn't be a very dignified name for your fancy, schmancy instrument."

"It was her childhood nickname, from Lilly-Alice. We all slip up and call her that sometimes. I don't know what it'll end up being. Ma wants it to have something to do with love and romance, but if things between Alice and me don't work out..."

"They'll work out," said Fort. "You're one of those guys who never falls for a woman until he really, *really* falls."

"Yeah, you're like those penguins that only imprint on one partner for their entire life. You're going to spend the next fifty years wandering around a proverbial rookery with rocks in your mouth to bring to Alice's nest."

"Dev, you're such a freak," said Fort. He turned back to me. "Speaking of penguins with rocks in their mouths, Dev's started the ring shopping process."

I slapped my blond, wisecracking friend on the back. "You don't say? They all fall like dominoes. Congratulations, man. Does Ella know?"

He shrugged, smiled. His paler skin did show a blush. "She probably knows. We're at the point where things aren't in question. But how do you find a rock to impress an astrophysicist girlfriend who probes the mysteries of the entire universe?"

"You said probes." I snickered.

"I'm sure she'll love whatever you get her, considering the connections you have to Sinclair Jewelers," said Fort, raising an eyebrow.

The waiter came to take our order, and we tried to talk about other things, but the conversation kept coming around to our girlfriends—and fiancées.

"You know," I pointed out. "Our five-years-ago selves would have been disgusted with us."

"Yeah, well, our five-years-ago selves were knee deep in debauchery at The Gallery," Fort said.

"Those were the growing years," Dev mused as a joke.

"The growth of our debauchery," Fort agreed.

"Alice has been asking me about The Gallery," I blurted out. "Well, ever since your gossipy submissives tried to 'help me out' by telling her about it." I rubbed the back of my neck, staring down at my mostly rare steak. "I'm not sure what to do."

"You mean, whether to take her?" Fort asked after a moment. "Do you think it would be too much for her?"

"She's really just started this journey."

"Yeah," Dev laughed. "But she started it with *you*. It's not like Ella and Jules didn't warn her about every damn thing from the start. My feeling is, if she's interested in going, you'll probably need to sate her curiosity."

Fort shrugged. "It's a good place to connect, to grow closer as a kinky couple. I'm sure if you brought her, she'd enjoy the experience. You'd know how to make it work for her."

"Yeah." My lips tightened into a line. "She's game to try anything. Maybe that's why I'm nervous."

Fort and Dev looked at each other, then Dev spoke up. "Maybe we could all go, you know, to offer moral support. Ella always enjoys it."

"Juliet does too," said Fort. "And if they were there, it might make Alice more comfortable during her first time. And Dev and I could be there in case, you know..."

In case something awful happens. In case you take shit too far. In an atmosphere as intense as The Gallery, things occasionally went wrong. Very wrong. As it happened, the two men across from me knew that from personal experience.

"Well, I'll think about it. We're still discussing the possibility," I said.

In the flush of our dawning relationship, since she'd taken to masochism so naturally, I'd been excited about introducing her to The

Gallery. Early on, I'd taken her to Michelle to be fitted for the requisite uniform, but going through that process with someone I cared about so deeply... It wasn't the same as fitting out other girls. I started having second thoughts.

Of course, by then, Alice was beside herself with excitement about the whole perverse secret-club thing, and assumed it was just a matter of time until we went there together. I loved The Gallery—it was such a fundamental part of my life and identity, but when it came to Alice, I was torn. I wanted to take her, but I didn't want anything between us to change. I didn't want the pathos and violence of The Gallery to scare her off the path we'd embarked on together.

"He's not listening to you," said Dev, drawing me from my thoughts and anxieties.

"What? Huh?" I shoved a piece of steak in my mouth, pretending I was only preoccupied by the food.

"I asked what your parents think of you and Alice getting together," said Fort, "considering how long you've been family friends?"

"Oh, Jesus. They don't know we're together yet. Like, carnally together. They think we're still friends. Otherwise, they'd never allow her to stay at my apartment. They'd make her move to Chappaqua so they could shelter her from immoral urges," I said, laughing.

"It cracks me up that your parents are so traditional."

"Wait," said Devin. "You said your mom wanted a love-and-romance name for the violin."

"Yeah, because they want us to fall in love. They've wanted it forever."

"So why don't you tell them?" Fort said. "They'll be so excited."

"I can't. Blue would lose his shit if she had to move out."

"You're both in your thirties," said Dev with a snort. "I don't think your parents can make either of you do anything you don't want to do."

"You don't know my parents. Or hers. Her dad is this hulking Swedish type that I'm still scared of from my violin-lesson days."

148

"You're a mess." Fort topped off my glass with the last of the wine. "Well, let us know about The Gallery. I know Juliet's been missing it, and would love to go. If we all went, it would be a lot of fun, and Dev and I could run interference on all the pervs who were interested in the new girl."

All the pervs. Fuck. That was the only thing about taking my new love to The Gallery. I'd shared women all my life, including dozens with Devin and Fort, but the idea of sharing Alice made my nerves go tight. Sharing had always been the height of kinky abandon for me, and Alice got off on the idea too, but what if I couldn't do it?

I looked across the table at my friends, seeing them as rivals and interlopers for the first time. I tried to keep my thoughts from showing on my face, but I wasn't sure I was successful, because Fort and Dev both buried their faces in the dessert menu, and we never, ever ordered dessert.

CHAPTER SIXTEEN: ALICE

I checked the app on my phone, making sure I was going the right direction on Broome Street. Michelle's studio wasn't that far from Ella's loaner apartment.

I had the uniform she'd made me tucked into the handbag under my arm. Lord knew the wispy thing didn't take up a whole lot of space. It was beautiful though, and it fit perfectly. Michelle was a skilled costumer for the Met Ballet, and it showed in the quality of the seams and trim. There was just one problem: my legs turned out to be too long for the standard stockings she provided. She'd special-ordered some for me, and I'd asked if I could come pick them up, since I needed them by tonight.

Oh my God. Tonight.

I wanted to go to The Gallery. It was important for me to take this next step, to experiment with my sex-kitten persona. It brought me joy, and it thrilled the man I loved. When I modeled the uniform for him—sans stockings—he'd jumped all over me, squeezing my ass, running his tongue along the silver collar's edge. As moments went, it was right up there with the night he showed me my finished violin.

Ah, my violin. It was beautiful, marvelous, perfect, but it still needed a name before I was allowed to register it for insurance, and play it publicly. I would have chosen *I love you so much oh my God Milo I can't believe I'm holding this amazing piece of wonder in my hands*, but that was kind of long for Fierro's records, and anyway, Luciana Fierro had the final choice, which she'd promised to make next week when we visited. I didn't know why she was taking so long. I'd played the instrument for hours every night since he'd given it to me, sometimes naked, at his request.

I'd come to love catering to his requests.

I found Michelle's building and rang up. As she escorted me into her workshop, I felt the same illicit thrill I'd felt the first time, when Milo had brought me to be measured. She was a kind, businesslike, slightly older lady, but her workshop would always feel like a hot-as-hell sex den to me.

"It's wonderful to see you again," she said with a smile. "Thanks for coming by to pick these up. Did you bring the rest of the uniform, so we can make sure everything fits?"

"Yes, I've got it here. Should I change into it?"

"Please, if you don't mind. Can I get you something to drink?"

"No, I'm fine. Thank you."

I shed my top and put on the bra first, arranging my nipples within the peekaboo cups. It made me think of Milo's obsession with hurting them, and my nipples went rock hard in response. I slipped off my panties next, while she puttered around with a coffee machine, perhaps to give me a sense of privacy in her wide-open workroom. Not that I'd have any privacy at The Gallery, from the official page of rules he'd shown me.

Number one: All submissives must be accompanied by a sponsor who will manage their conduct and care. No unsponsored submissives will be admitted.

Number two: Any submissive brought into The Gallery shall be considered communal property and shared in any way her sponsor desires.

Number three: The Gallery is a no-safe-word zone. The submissive's limits will be determined by her sponsor.

Number four: All submissives must strictly adhere to The Gallery's dress code.

Number five: Any submissive not agreeing to these terms may not be admitted to The Gallery. Any resistance or refusal of these rules is cause for immediate expulsion from the premises.

"Almost ready?" asked Michelle as I finished buckling on the last thing—the collar. She slid an approving look over the bra and garter belt, which flattered my angular body shape. "Aren't you a tall, graceful beauty? Let's try those stockings. I'd kill to have your legs."

I stepped into the soft, silken stockings and pulled them up my legs, then stopped. "Can you help me work these things?"

"The stocking clasps? Sure. They're easier to use than they look, especially when the stockings are the right length." She showed me how to attach the decorative clasps to the upper parts of the stockings, lining them up so the suspenders laid straight. When that was accomplished, she straightened and nodded in approval. "You see, it looks so much better when the stockings are the right length, because they don't pull down on the garter belt and ruin the balance."

I clasped my hands in front of my waist, excited, embarrassed, and happy at once. "Thank you so much."

"My pleasure. Would you like to see the whole outfit? Well, except for the shoes. They'll make your legs even longer. Milo will be so pleased."

She turned her standing mirror so it caught my reflection. I stared at myself, at pale skin and black lines crossing over it. My face looked scared. I laughed as soon as I noticed it.

"I'm nervous," I confessed. "I've never been to a BDSM club, much less a private, exclusive one."

"Oh, a lot of the women I outfit are nervous," she said kindly. "Then I see them at The Gallery a few weeks later having a grand old time. And Milo's a fun one to go with. He's known for his creative mind."

This woman knew more about Milo playing at The Gallery than I did, but not for long. He might be nervous about taking me there, about how I would react, but all I wanted was to know everything about him, the good, the bad, the normal, the weird, the scary. "Honestly, I'm not even sure he wants me to go," I confessed, "but I don't want him to feel like he's keeping secrets from me, or that he has to hide what he's into."

"Well, you've read the rules, haven't you?" I nodded and she smiled. "So you know what he's into. What about you? Are you a masochist as well as a submissive? Are you into pain?"

"Yes, definitely. Well, not all pain. Just sexy pain."

"Everything's sexy at The Gallery," she assured me. "I think you'll have a transformative time there."

"I hope so. I think I will." I took a final look in the mirror, touching the collar at my neck. "I guess I should take this off now."

"I wouldn't wear it home, if that's what you're asking. Here, hand it to me as you take it off, and I'll fold it up so it stays nice for tonight."

When I left a few minutes later, my uniform was once again tucked in my handbag. I had a concert to play with Met Orchestra tonight, and we'd go to The Gallery afterward. As far as I knew, his friends were meeting us there, but beyond that, I had no idea what would go down. I didn't want to build up any hopes—or fears. As long as Milo was with me, everything would be okay.

CHAPTER SEVENTEEN:
MILO

I leaned against the counter, watching Alice primp for the evening. She was fresh out of the shower, applying makeup in the nude. It took everything I had not to molest her as she leaned over to put on black eyeliner. I needed to save those urges for The Gallery, or we'd end up very late.

"Is that eyeliner waterproof?" I asked.

She looked at the tube. "I don't know."

I hoped it wasn't. There was something about messy, running eyeliner as your masochist submissive broke down in tears. When she finished the eyeliner, she put on some crimson-red lipstick, and I wanted to fuck her mouth so badly. I wondered if this whole leisurely makeup process was meant as a tease.

"What should I do with my hair?" she asked. "Leave it loose so you can grab it?"

"No, braid it for me. You know, that thing where you wrap the braids around your head?" I motioned over the crown of my dark hair. "It excites me when you have that innocent-Heidi look."

"That 'innocent-Heidi look'? You're a pervert."

"Maybe. When I see those braids around your head, all I can think about is taking them down and doing nefarious things to them."

"Hair pervert," she muttered, but she humored me and picked up her comb. She loved humoring my whims, and it made my life a fucking dream. After she braided her hair with quick, deft finger movements, she squirmed into her Gallery uniform. The sexually overt costume had featured prominently in my dreams ever since she'd tried it on for me. I got hard watching her pull up the stockings. "Here, Cinderella," I said, picking up the stilettos. "Allow me."

She held onto my shoulders as I slipped the first shoe on her foot, then the second. When she stood, she almost reached my height. Almost.

"You're so beautiful," I said. "So ridiculously beautiful."

She smiled and straightened my tie, then ran a hand along my suit coat's lapel. I was in formal business attire, because the Doms at The Gallery had a dress code too.

"You're ridiculously beautiful as well, Milo Fierro. Oh, I still need my collar."

"Let me do it."

I'd wanted to put on her shoes because I loved her feet and her elegant calf muscles. I wanted to put on her collar because she belonged to me. I was more certain of it every day. *Mine. My woman, forever and ever.* Even so, her collar, like all the women's collars at the club, had a dangling, decorative lock that read *Property of The Gallery*.

It was okay. She could belong to me, and still play with others at The Gallery. I'd have to work that out. Once we were in the thick of things, in the passionate violence of the main dungeon, I'd most likely be able to share her to a reasonable extent. Passing willing women around was just kink, fun stuff, and I trusted every Dom there to take care of her and follow the rules.

"The silver-toned leather looks nice on you," I said. "You were made to wear a collar."

She put a hand over mine. "I wouldn't have thought that a couple months ago, but now..."

I took her chin and pulled her close for a kiss. She braced against me until she found her footing in the stilettos, then my other hand traced down the straps framing her ass. It was so lovely, so round and beautiful. I groaned into Alice's mouth.

"We should go," I said. "Otherwise we won't get there at all."

I went to the closet to get her fitted black coat that ended just above her knees. She couldn't go up on the elevator without it, even though I hated covering up her sexy outfit, even for a moment. As she tied the belt closed in front of her, I hugged her from behind, pressing my cheek to hers.

"You're sure you want to do this?" I asked. "We don't have to. We can wait a little longer."

"The longer I wait, the more anxious I get about going. So let's go." She reached to stroke my cheek. "I'm sure it will be great, and if I don't like it, I'll tell you."

"You promise?"

She turned her head to kiss me, then said, "I promise, Sir."

We got into the elevator and rode it up to the top floor, to the clock tower that had been renovated into a three-level wonderland for sadomasochistic play. The doors opened into the lobby, and I smiled at her delighted intake of breath. It was a gorgeous, soaring space, with ornate molding and eighteenth century reproduction iron sconces lining the walls, making the gilded, flocked wallpaper glint in the low light.

"It's so beautiful," she said.

"I think so too." Even so, it wasn't as beautiful as her, with her shining eyes and shapely, scarlet lips. Rene, a young man who served as both greeter and security, smiled at us.

"Welcome to The Gallery, Mr. Fierro."

"Good evening, Rene. This is Alice. She'll be joining us tonight for the first time."

"That's wonderful. Welcome, Alice," he said with his typical smooth elegance. "I'll be happy to take your coats, and then I'll have a document for you to sign."

I helped take off her coat, enjoying the small, anxious shiver that came as I lifted it from her shoulders and exposed her to Rene's avid gaze. He had no sexual interest in women, so her charms wouldn't arouse him, but he did raise a perfectly plucked brow in appreciation. She looked like an ancient Greek statue, tall, curvaceous, voluptuous, womanly, built for sex. I noted with pleasure that her nipples were tightly erect.

As soon as Rene completed his check of her uniform, he offered the submissive's contract for her to sign. Alice accepted the paper and scanned the five rules she needed to agree to. We'd gone over them in detail already—when she was calm and thoughtful, and not in the throes of kinky ecstasy—because I wanted her to know what she was getting into. After a cursory reading, she put her signature at the bottom and handed it back to Rene, and we were waved toward the large gold and ivory door that led to the dungeon.

"Things are already in full swing," Rene said. "There's a crowd tonight. Enjoy."

"I'm sure we will." I turned to Alice. "Ready?"

"Yes, Sir," she said in a soft voice. "Let's do this."

I gave her ass an encouraging squeeze as I opened the door and led her up the circular staircase to the main dungeon. The sound of sex and pleasure—as well as the shrieks and groans of masochism—flooded our ears before we even reached the top. As we came to the landing, Alice paused, holding onto the banister for support.

I let her look a moment. She'd never been to a mainstream BDSM club, much less a private dungeon, so for her, there was a lot to take in. The Gallery rose to a grand dome overhead, and featured several scening areas with professional-grade bondage furniture and racks, as well as couches and chairs where members chatted, cuddled, or fucked. The lights in the dungeon were dim enough to suggest eroticism and mystery, but bright enough to showcase lots of naked, glistening skin, stark bondage equipment, and polished leather implements.

"What do you think?" I asked, as she stood frozen beside me.

"It's so amazing. I can't believe this is real." She watched some cavorting couples nearby, then lifted her gaze to the balcony above us, and the large, frosted glass clock face on the wall, half obscured by interlocking gears. "That clock...it's huge. Look how it glows."

"It's pretty, isn't it?" I'd always loved to play in the light of that glow. "Unfortunately, it hasn't worked for some time, and no one's been able to fix it."

She'd moved on from looking at the clock, to gawk at the various groups playing on the main dungeon floor. "Oh." She made a small, shocked sound. "There's Ella and Devin."

Ella was straddling Dev's lap on the couch farthest away from us, both of them doing some raw, animalistic fucking as they gazed into each other's eyes. From the looks of Ella's butt cheeks, she'd already endured a strapping or paddling—or both.

"Come on," I said. The longer Alice stood there, fingering her collar, the more nervous she'd get. I decided to take her to a rack near the back of the room, not because I wanted to hide her...

Well, maybe I wanted to hide her. Other Doms were starting to notice her. Even Devin tore his gaze away from Ella for a moment to give me a distracted thumbs up. Damn it. Alice was too striking for the others not to notice, and she broadcast "newbie" and "innocent" on top of it. Maybe I shouldn't have insisted on the braids.

I tried to push the jealous thoughts out of my head. That wasn't why we'd come here. I needed to tease and torment her, and show her what The Gallery was all about. The other Doms could fuck themselves, because this was Alice's journey. I led my wide eyed submissive to a square-shaped rack, so I could put those long legs to use. It was designed with sturdy posts and a top and bottom bar, so the victim could be bound facing either direction. I decided to cuff her facing outward to the dungeon, so she could see the other scenes, and understand that she'd become part of this secret, depraved world.

I soon realized my mistake. After I bound her arms, and spread her legs impossibly, obscenely wide, cuffing them to either side of the rack, she made too desperate and too beautiful a picture. Men started drifting over, some of them with their submissives in tow.

The old Milo would have been proud to show off a bound, scared submissive, her tight nipples thrusting from her peekaboo bra, but the new Milo who was in love with Alice wanted to shout at all of them to go away. One of them moved toward her in a manner that would have been perfectly acceptable with any of my other partners. He gave her hard nipples an appreciative pinch. "Going to use clamps? I'd be happy to help with that."

Alice looked at him, then at me. This was turning her on, I could see it in her gaze. She was willing, perhaps even enjoying the attention. She trusted me to engineer the scene, to make everything okay. She was fine.

But I wasn't fine. My fists clenched at my sides.

Fort appeared, jolting me from my frozen moment of fury. He touched Alice—barely—running a hand along her side. "She looks beautiful, man," he said in a quiet voice. "How's everything going?"

I forced my gritted teeth to part. "Not so good."

"Juliet and I could join you two if you like, and shoulder out some of the others. Or would you rather go?"

I stared at Fort a moment, thought about the cane I wanted to fetch, the way I wanted to hurt Alice and then hold her close to me. In my mind's eye, it was just her and me. I didn't want anyone else to touch her.

I couldn't let anyone else touch her.

"I don't think I can do this." My voice sounded hoarse.

"Hey, man, it's okay. I'll help you unbind her."

"No, I can do it."

"Great." He turned away, looking toward the small group that had gathered. He didn't say anything; his expression was sufficient to make them back off. He left too, so it was just me and Alice, and my trembling fingers unbinding her.

"What's wrong?" she asked. "Why are we stopping?"

Her eyes looked a little shiny, and her voice wavered. *Please don't cry. Don't be upset. I'm the one who can't do this.*

"Let's go back down to my place," I said. "I'd rather play there."

"Yes, Sir."

Rene made no comment when we emerged from the ivory door a mere fifteen minutes after we'd entered it. He got my coat and then Alice's coat, and chose not to react when I snatched it from his fingers, unwilling to let even him approach my woman. I knew I was being ridiculous. The Gallery was a place for sharing. That was why a lot of people joined up here, when they could have just played at home. It was a place for reveling jointly in shared, perverse sexuality.

But not with Alice. Nope. I thought I could handle sharing her, but it wasn't going to work.

CHAPTER EIGHTEEN: ALICE

The look on Milo's face worried me. That fact that he wouldn't look at me scared me to my soul. We rode down on the elevator without words. I wanted to reach for his hand, but I didn't know if he'd take it or push it away. It wasn't until we entered his apartment that he turned to me and let out a sigh.

"I'm sorry, baby. I know you wanted to play there."

I studied him, trying to understand his mood. He was like an alarm about to go off. I took a step closer, holding his gaze. "Well, why can't we? What did Fort say? What happened up there?"

"What happened?" His gaze darted around the room before it fixed back on me. "What happened is that I'm in love with you. Not friendship love. Not new relationship love in the blush of spring. Not kinky love, where I can take you to The Gallery and share you. I'm hardcore, freaked-out in love with you. I'm in love with you to the point that it's...it's changing who I am."

He forced out the last words. My heart beat fast and hard with excitement—he was really in love with me—but he didn't seem like he was handling it very well. "What do you mean, it's changing who you are? You seem the same to me, Milo."

"No, I'm changing." He stalked away from me, took off his suit jacket and threw it over the couch with enough force to wake Blue from his lazy-dog slumber. He looked up at us, his liquid eyes curious. Milo gave him a quick pat, then turned back to me. "I've always been a man unto myself, Alice. I loved you from far away, and nothing had to change. Now I can't sleep without you beside me. I can't let you play any violin but the one I made for you. I can't let anyone else touch you. When that guy touched you..." His voice had been rising, but now it fell to a near whisper. "Jesus, I wanted to break his neck. And I'm not like that. With me, it's always been share and share alike." His gaze pinned me with hot fervor. "But I can't share you."

"You don't have to share me. There's nothing wrong with that. And there's nothing wrong with changing." I crossed to Blue's bed and crouched to stroke his ears. "Look at Blue here. He used to run around a track while people bet on him. Now he only wakes up to eat or be petted. He's still a wonderful boy, even though he's changed a lot." I leaned down and touched my nose to his. "Aren't you, Bluebeard? You're still our sweet little villain, killing all your wives."

"Huh?"

I glanced at Milo. "Didn't you look up the legend of Bluebeard after you adopted him? It's pretty grisly. There's a secret dungeon in the story, and lots of dead wives. Not sure I'd accept a marriage proposal from you," I joked, addressing the dog again. But Blue was easy to face, and to joke with. Milo, not so much.

"Are you angry?" I asked, still uncertain of his mood.

"No, I'm not angry. I'm just unsettled."

"Unsettled. That's a good word." I stood and drew my coat closer around me, pulling at the tie that held it closed. "I just want to be what you want, Milo. I was interested in playing at The Gallery, but if you don't want to..."

"It's not that I don't want to. I want to be there with you, to teach you things and show you off to everyone, but I can't, because I can't follow the rules anymore. I can't stand for you to be *communal property*." He reached behind my neck to unbuckle my collar, and showed me the lock. "I designed this *Property of the Gallery* shit, but with you and me, it's not going to work."

"Well, what does that mean for us?" I took his hand before he wrenched off the lock. "What do you want more? Being with me, or keeping your life the way it was before? Loving me..." It hurt to say the next words. "Or loving me from a distance? I'm the one who pressed you for this relationship, but if you truly don't want it, that's also okay."

He stared at me like I was speaking some other language. "I could never go back to loving you from a distance, not now that you've been so close."

"Good." I ran my fingers down the front of his tie. "Because as long as you want me, I'll be here, even if you have to...well...change a little bit." I looked up at him from beneath my lashes. "But will you still hurt me? Can you still make me cry so you can kiss it better? Cause there's a dungeon right here," I reminded him, gesturing toward the hall. "Maybe we can go there, and you can bind me up again with my legs spread wide, because I love that side of you, Milo Fierro, and I always will."

He seemed to snap out of whatever dread or anxiety held him. He reached out to me, pulling at the coat's sash. "Yes. Let's go to the dungeon. Let's pick up where we left off."

"I'd like that," I said, happiness filling my voice.

We went down the hall to his L-shaped chamber, which wasn't as large or busy as The Gallery, but every bit as thrilling, because he was there. As we paused inside the door, his dark gaze roved my body like a caress.

"I want to hurt you so much," he said, and I knew what he really meant was *I love you so much.* Now that we were here, alone, the nervous edge had left his movements. He crossed back and forth, gathering what he needed and placing it beside a rack that was very similar in design to the one he'd put me on at The Gallery. Cuffs, clover clamps, spreader bar, lube, and a thin rattan cane. It didn't look like much equipment, but I knew what he could do with them.

"Let's get you in the right headspace before we begin. Kneel down," he said in his commanding Dom voice.

As he undid his pants, I fell to my knees, opening my lips to accept his already-hardening cock. Since we'd gotten STD tests done, we didn't use condoms for oral anymore. I loved having the warm, natural taste of him in my mouth, rather than the chemical taste of latex. When he shoved deep, making me gag, it didn't seem quite so bad.

I still cried, though. I was working on my deep throating skills, but I wasn't the best at it yet. Milo made encouraging sounds when I choked, and kept me at my task by grasping my crown of braids. After a few minutes, my hair started coming down, and he released me so I could catch my breath. He took off his pants and fisted his scary-hard cock, as I collected the hairpins from the floor.

"Give them to me," he said, then looked at one a little too closely. "I wonder how this would feel attached to your clit?"

I wiped at the tears his hard facefucking had dislodged, and clamped my legs together. I didn't think it would feel good at all. I watched in dismay as he inspected the bobby pin's edges. "These are coated, so they don't have sharp edges. Lie back for me, Alice, and open your legs."

Shit, shit, shit. He knelt between my legs and ran his hands up my silken stockings, then down to my stilettos.

"Put the bottom of your shoes on the floor and keep them there. No kicking and squirming around."

To my relief, he was bending the bobby pin a little, so it wouldn't be on me "full strength."

"Part your pussy lips," he said when he was done. "I'm going to need two hands for this delicate maneuver."

He used two hands *and* his mouth, sucking at the folds of my sex, revealing my rapidly swelling clit. I threw my head back when he dragged his tongue across the sensitive button.

"That feels good, doesn't it?"

"Yes, Sir."

"You taste delicious, wicked and sweet. What's pleasure, though, without pain?"

He positioned the hairpin over my clit and slid it carefully onto the engorged, throbbing nub. The pain was immediate, and nearly unbearable in my heightened state of arousal.

"Oh... Oww..." I bucked my hips, taking care to keep my shoes flat on the floor as he'd told me. He stood above me, watching me suffer for a moment, pure delight on his face. I squeezed out a few more tears, blinking through the pain.

"I won't leave it on forever," he said, helping me up. "Although we might look into some intimate piercings in the near future. That might be fun."

"Yes, Sir," I breathed, tottering on my heels.

He backed me up to the rack with a stare that had me shivering. My legs were bound first, spread apart. My poor clit ached as the air caressed it. "How... How long...?" I began in a quivery voice.

"As long as I think you need. Arms up, please."

I swallowed. He bound my wrists to the top of the rack, spread as wide as my legs. My breasts were exposed, along with my pussy, by The Gallery uniform. I stretched my body, trying to get comfortable since I couldn't get away. Honestly, I didn't want to get away, even when he picked up the hated clover clamps. But as he turned and saw the suffering on my face, he paused.

"If I'm going to clamp your clit with a hairpin, I might as well use them for your nipples too. It'll provide a nice circle of continuity."

Continuity? More like agony. Ugh, why had I used so many pins in my hair? I should have known my crown of braids wouldn't survive this night intact. He took two of the pins he'd collected earlier and bent them open, just a little, as he'd done with the one he put on my clit. Like that one, these pins hurt like hell when he applied them. They gripped my nipples like little shark mouths, and no way were they coming off unless he bent them off.

"Ow, it really hurts, Sir." I squirmed to try to soothe the pain, but it only turned him on more. He shed the rest of his clothes and kicked off his boxers. Tall, beautiful, strong Milo, ready to hurt and fuck me. He stood in front of me and lifted my chin, gazing into my teary eyes.

"Do you remember the safe word, baby?"

"I don't need a safe word," I said. "This is our Gallery. Let's not depend on safe words, because I know you'll keep me safe."

I could tell my request touched him. I could also tell he wasn't sure about the idea. "I'm going to use a cane on you, Alice. Canes really hurt. Then I'm going to fuck your ass without plugging you first. You sure you don't want that safe word?"

I shook my head, excited and terrified. "No, Sir."

He studied me a moment, then turned away, picking up his tie from the chair where he'd laid it. At first I thought he'd blindfold me, but then I remembered him saying that blindfolds weren't allowed when safe words weren't used, like in The Gallery. *The eyes say more than safe words ever could*, he'd told me, *if the Dom's paying attention.*

No, he used his tie as a gag instead, shoving it between my lips and tying it tightly behind my head. I could breathe, but talking was out. When he finished tying it off, he gave it a little shake, and my whole body trembled. I was bound and speechless, utterly helpless in his hands.

"These little pins hurt, I bet," he said, flicking my nipples. When I nodded, he offered dubious comfort: "I won't leave them on too long. It doesn't take that many strokes to break someone down with a cane. But after, when I fuck you..." His lips curved in a sadistic smile. "I'll make that last a long, long time before I let you come."

I moaned. It sounded strange and muffled behind the gag, and so erotic. I'd never been gagged before, so I moaned again to get used to the sound. Milo walked behind me and I felt the cane tap against my ass. He'd never used one on me before, so I wasn't sure what to expect, but I knew it wouldn't be pleasant.

Not. Pleasant. At. All. Owww. When the first stroke came, I yowled at the shocking, blistering sting. Now my muffled voice sounded strangled. He waited a moment, steadying me with a hand on my waist. *How many?* I wanted to beg. *How many of these do I have to take? This really hurts!*

Instead I could only groan as another blow fell. It was just a small flick of his wrist. I could see the movement if I turned my head, but then everything went fuzzy when the thin, whippy implement connected. Three strokes. Four. A sob escaped my throat, and drool started soaking through my improvised gag. If I didn't ruin his tie with saliva, I'd ruin it with tears.

"Take a breath," he said, slapping my face to catch my attention. When I crooned behind the gag, he did it again, a little smile curving the edges of his lips. "Everything's okay. You can't get away, right? Just take the pain, let it empty you out so there's more room for my cock." As he gazed at me, he spanked the four sore welts that throbbed in the center of my ass cheeks. I danced on my toes, mewling in protest, but I kept my eyes on his, because his expression was so warm, so beautiful and challenging.

"You're my brave girl, aren't you?"

I nodded, hoping he wouldn't slap my face again, but kind of wanting him to slap me again. He spanked my ass instead, several hard smacks in succession as I wailed against the gag. The spanking was a different kind of pain from the caning, but still hot and cruel on my sore butt. He kissed my face, my nose and eyes, his lips coming away wet with tears. "You're a beautiful crier," he said, making me look at him. "We're almost done, baby. Can you take four more?"

I didn't think I could. I had no answer to give him, just the frantic tensing of my muscles.

"Okay," he murmured. "We'll see."

The next stroke landed near the curve of my ass. I grasped the cuffs holding my hands and squealed behind the gag. It hurt so badly. Pure sadism, no pleasure. I understood that he needed that kind of sadism to get off, so I let my tears flow as the last three strokes came. I wailed and struggled, forgetting the biting pain at my clit and nipples because my ass hurt so, so bad.

He put down the cane after the last stroke and held me around the waist, kissing me, poking his cock against the hairpin on my clit, making it throb in concert with my wrecked ass. My butt cheeks felt like they were exploding, the heat and pain was so agonizing. He spanked each one again, hard and fast, to make things worse, or maybe to help diffuse the pain over a greater surface. Everything hurt. Everything felt squeezed and stung and punished by him.

After he watched me cry another moment, he eased the hairpin off my clit. I was so wet, it slid off easily, but it left plenty of sensitivity behind. "Poor baby," Milo said, stroking the swollen button. "That was so mean. We'll leave your clit alone the next few days, yes? So it can get better?" He laughed at my whine of protest. "And I'll only fuck your ass, since your clit's out of commission. Maybe we'll go anal-only for a whole month."

I gave him my most forlorn look, but my pussy pulsed at the picture his crass words painted. Anal-only would hurt. It would be dirty and naughty, the perfect way for a sadist Dom to torment his submissive.

"Don't worry," he said. "I'll still let you come, if you can learn to do it from assfucking alone."

As I moaned, he took the hairpins off my nipples. He squeezed and licked my breasts where they jutted from my bra, blowing hot air across them. My nipples were still hard, still ready for more abuse. He pinched them as he teased my clit some more, sliding his cock between my legs. I was still in pain, yes, but I was getting hot as hell at the same time. I moved my hips forward and whined behind the gag.

He reached above me to release my arms. "I told you, Alice, I'm not fucking your pussy tonight. Your ass is so red and striped. It makes your asshole a much more inviting target."

The first thing I did when my hands were free was reach behind me to rub my sore butt, even though it was forbidden. Milo pushed them away from the throbbing welts. "No. If you want to do something with those hands, hold your ass cheeks open so I can lube you up. Or would you rather forgo lubrication?"

I made a frantic sound of denial, and he grabbed the bottle, liberally greasing my asshole. I could feel just from the pressure of his fingertips how tight I was, probably from the pain of my caning. He shoved a couple fingers in anyway, pushing the lube deep, making me squirm and moan behind the gag as he stretched me open.

When he was done, he guided me down onto my hands and knees, with my ankles still braced wide by the bar. It was an incredibly exposing position, especially knowing that Milo was behind me, preparing to invade my ass. He didn't make me wait for it to happen. Holding my hip with one hand, and his cock with the other, he probed my tight hole.

I was supposed to be submissive to him, and I tried, but I couldn't stay perfectly still as he pushed into me. I tensed and moved my ass to one side, but he made a scolding sound and pressed a little deeper. Now it really hurt. We had anal on a pretty frequent basis, so I was learning to deal with his size, but I didn't think I'd ever get used to the aching stretch and feeling of lost control at the beginning.

"Oh, please," I whispered, even though the gag made it impossible for him to hear me. "Please stop hurting."

As always, just when I thought I couldn't bear the pressure a moment longer, my muscles relaxed enough to let him slide in. It went from an ache to a deep, shivering surrender, and the deeper he entered, the more subjugated I felt. My legs strained and spread wider, and my back arched to let him drive deeper. He growled in approval, holding the tails of his tie so the gag dug into the sides of my mouth.

"*Unh, unh, unh.*" I made desperate sounds, arousal taking over any civilized words. He arched over me from behind, taking my ass, thrusting steadily inside me. His fingers found the tips of my breasts and tugged on my sore nipples, reviving that pain, but making it more exciting. I was glad for the generous lube when he started pounding me faster, shoving me forward until I collapsed, legs spread, arms splayed to the sides. He grabbed my wrists and held me so I was pinned down completely, unable to escape.

I don't want to escape, though. I never want to escape.

His thrusting hips banged into my welted butt cheeks, another layer of masochistic sensation that had me speeding toward orgasm. I hadn't developed the ability to come yet from anal alone, but if I tilted my hips, I could grind my pussy against the floor, enough that my clit would send me over the edge. His hand moved from my nipples to my neck, squeezing, taking the last layer of my control, my own breath.

"Oh God," I cried against the sodden tie in my mouth.

"I'm fucking you, baby. You're all mine. Do I feel good in your ass?"

"Yes, Sir. *Ow.*" I tried to squirm away from his grip, tried to get the words out past the gag. "I want to come."

As distorted as my plea was, he understood it from my desperation. "You have to come with me in your ass, Alice, and my hand on your throat. I control you. I own you. You're mine."

With every squeeze of his fingers, my ass clenched tighter. His own breath hissed out behind my ear. He was driving me against the floor, causing my splayed legs to tense with each thrust. I wasn't me anymore, I was *his* body, *his* vessel. He loved me and I loved him. *You're mine.* How many years had I dreamed of him saying that? I'd known it would be this way, a violent, passionate possession, not the polite love of other boyfriends.

Milo was more than a boyfriend. He was my soul.

The lust and fear inside me transformed into the edge of an orgasm, and my swollen clit sliding against the floor gave me the rest of the impetus I needed. I started to climax, my legs trembling and pulling in their bonds, my ass arching as I contracted around his pounding length. He collapsed over top of me, driving deep, his fingers nearly choking me in the process. The edges of my vision went black and I turned my head, whining. He released my neck and hugged my shoulders instead as he came in me with hard thrusts.

He went still on top of me, post-orgasm. "I'm sorry," he whispered, his hair tickling my cheek. "That was too hard."

"No," I said through the gag. He removed it for me, so I could take unobstructed breaths. I wiggled my tongue and said it again. "No, it wasn't too hard. I loved it."

"I could have hurt you that time."

"You'll never hurt me. You took care of me. But I might be a little sore tomorrow."

He pulled out of me and patted my welted ass as he sprawled beside me on the floor. "More than a little sore tomorrow. I have to take things slower. We can build to these kinds of sessions over time. Maybe we can even build to The Gallery." He frowned at me, his head propped on his hand. "I'm sorry I flipped out and dragged you out of there tonight."

I stroked his cheek. "You can't do this every time things get intense. You can't feel guilty for the things you do to me. You're not a monster or a predator. You're the man I love, and there's nowhere else I'd rather be than here on...on your dungeon floor." I looked down at my wrecked, exhausted limbs and laughed. "With my ankles bound and my chin full of gag drool, and my neck full of bruises."

"There won't be bruises," he said quickly. "I'll never choke you that hard."

We both laughed then. How many lovers had these kinds of conversations?

"Just don't worry so much," I told him. "I have a great time with you in this dungeon, even when things get intense. I've always wanted to be close to you, crazy close, even when we were kids and I didn't know what my feelings meant." I took his face and made him look at me. "So I love your roughness now. I love your edge, your passion. I love that you want to hurt me."

"You little pervert."

"I love it all, because I know you'll never hurt me too much. I want you to teach me, to train me to do even harder sessions than these. You started, and I want you to keep going. I want us to do this together, violent sexual urges and everything. It makes me feel very...well...very wanted and desired."

"You are very wanted and desired." He traced the lines of my Gallery uniform, over the garter belt lace and beading, and down the suspenders to the silk tops of my stockings. "And I love you for doing these things with me, Alice. I never would have thought you'd allow me to..." He gave a rueful laugh. "I'll get used to it. I'll get over the guilt thing." He sobered and kissed me, lingering over my lips. "I never thought I'd be able to debase you this way, and have you enjoy it, but you're full of mystery and surprises, Lala Nyquist. You've always accepted me as I am. Why would this be any different?"

"It's possible there was a secret masochist inside me, waiting to be let out."

He laughed, one of the loud, raucous laughs he rarely shared with the world. "I'm sure there was some masochist inside you. Otherwise you would have run far away from me by now." He traced my leg, down to my ankle, his beautiful lips pursed with a combination of embarrassment and joy. "I guess I should let you go."

"Maybe. As much as I enjoy playing in here with you, the floor gets kind of hard."

"We'll have some soft carpets installed," he joked, leaning to unbuckle the cuffs around my ankles. "Anything for my masochist's comfort." He took off one of my shoes with a whistle. "You did a number on these, baby."

The toes and sides of my patent leather stilettos were scuffed to the point of disaster. "I may have kicked around a little while you were riding my ass. I'm surprised the stockings made it through intact."

He took off the other shoe and looked at them together as I stretched my legs and sat up. "Well, we can get you another pair of stilettos if we ever want to go back to The Gallery."

"It's okay if you don't want to. Or..." I forced the words out, out of love for him. "If you had to go with someone else, you know, to do your sharing thing without me."

He was already shaking his head. "I don't have to go to The Gallery. You're more important in my mind."

"I just don't want you to feel like you're missing out."

"How could I feel that with you?" he asked, cupping my chin. His fingers strayed down to my neck, where he'd gripped me so possessively. "We'll be away next weekend anyway."

"I'm so excited for Italy," she said, her eyes shining. "And seeing the Fierro castle again."

"It's not a castle."

"I like to think of it as a castle. It's so stony and rocky and rugged." I took his hand as he helped me up. "Like you."

He held me against him and I buried my face in his neck, reveling in his warmth and scent, and the closeness I'd dreamed of for so long. "And I'm excited to play my violin for everyone," I added. "The violin with your heart."

He probably thought I meant the heart he'd hidden in the wood grain and varnish, and I did, but I also meant the heart of his efforts, building it to fit me perfectly. Everything about us fit perfectly, and the violin would always stand as a symbol of our love, even if we fell out of love, or didn't stay together.

But that wouldn't happen. I held him tighter, drifting in his protective embrace, listening to the steady beat of his heart.

CHAPTER NINETEEN: MILO

I went to The Gallery on my Monday lunch break to meet with Fort about the clock. He claimed he could fix it, even though it had stubbornly resisted working for years. It was strange to walk through the rococo lobby during daylight, without Rene manning the door. I let myself into the inner sanctum, winding up the stairs, hearing only silence rather than the screams and moans of normal Gallery operation.

"I'm over here," Fort called as I appeared. He was doing pull-ups on the square rack I'd attempted to use over the weekend. He jumped down and crossed the empty dungeon floor. "Just checking the racks for stability."

"It'd take an earthquake to bring those down. The clock, on the other hand..."

"It's going to work this time. I'm sure I figured out the problem, and I measured the part twice. More like seventeen times. Those hands are about to move, brother."

"Awesome. Can't wait for you to work your Sinclair magic." I looked up at the scaffolding structure Fort had erected to reach the clock. "You're sure that'll hold you?"

"If it doesn't, it's your job to catch me." He held out a small cardboard box and opened the lid. "This is the piece, man. This is the part you needed all this time. Once it's in there, that clock's going to keep perfect time."

"From your lips to God's ears." It was one of my mother's favorite sayings, an incantation for when you really wanted things to work out. "Do you need me to hold the bottom of the scaffolding to keep it steady?"

"I borrowed it from a friend in construction, and he helped me put it together. Everything's going to be okay."

"Because The Gallery doesn't carry workplace-accident insurance."

"Why the fuck not?" He laughed and shoved the cardboard box in his pocket, and started scaling the outside of the scaffold structure. True to his word, it seemed sturdy, barely swaying under Fort's muscular bulk.

"That toolbelt's pretty sexy, man," I said, looking up at him. "What do you have in there? Your engraver? Your needle punches? A petite metal solder?"

"I do have a metal solder, jackass, and some wrenches and screwdrivers. Do you want me to fix the clock or not?"

I waved my hand in apology—jewelers' tools were so *petite*—and looked around the empty club. So many horny memories, and one really disturbing one. I wished I could enjoy The Gallery together with Alice, but I was apparently too jealous and possessive. "Fuck," I muttered to myself.

"What?" asked Fort. Every sound echoed in the quiet dungeon.

"Nothing," I replied.

I heard a grinding noise, an alarming clang, and a curse from Fort, but then he yelled down, "Everything's okay. Just getting in there."

"Yeah, you're good at that."

176

He laughed. "I try my best."

"Hey, how's the wedding planning coming along?" I didn't want to distract him from his work, but I also couldn't stand to look at the dungeon around me.

"Planning's going great," said Fort. "Going to be medium sized, lots of food, open bar, and Goodluck's insisted on doing the decorating."

"Holy crap."

"I know, it's going to be a riot." He looked down, his expression bemused, as it always was when we talked about Juliet's crazy boss. "He volunteered his cat, Mr. Snail Shell, to be the Best Man, but I told him the job was taken. I would have picked you but—"

"I know, you've known Devin longer."

"Yeah, and he'll probably give a jollier toast at the reception. You aren't known for your uplifting speeches, although you play a mean violin. Can you play during our service?"

"I'd be happy to."

"And Ella's going to be Juliet's Maid of Honor. Speaking of which, Dev's going to pop the question any day now. The lessons sealed the deal."

"What lessons?" Another loud clang was followed by a grinding sound, and I had to repeat my question. "What lessons?"

"Flying lessons, man. For *Ella*."

"No way."

"I swear to God, it's true."

"But she's petrified of flying. She always has been."

"Not anymore." Fort grunted, turning a gear and tugging it off the clock face's massive spindle. "She fell in love with a pilot, now she wants to do pilot-y things. People change."

There's nothing wrong with changing. That's what Alice had told me Saturday night. She'd changed me in so many ways over the past few weeks, I hardly recognized myself. "Who's giving her the lessons?" I asked. "Devin?"

"Yeah. He went back and forth in the beginning, didn't trust himself to do it. But in the end, he couldn't pass the responsibility off to someone else."

I stared up at the clock, watching it come to pieces. I trusted that Fort could put it back together; he was the son of one of the world's foremost jewelers, after all. He took the box from his pocket and removed the piece that was supposed to fix everything. It was hardly bigger than the tip of my thumb. He adjusted the work light belted to his head and leaned closer to study the clock's inner workings.

"Oh, yeah," he muttered to himself. I didn't know if it was a good or bad *oh, yeah*, and I didn't want to ask.

"Hey, Milo," he said as he fiddled with the clock's innards. "I meant to ask you about Saturday night. You and Alice cut out of here pretty quickly. Was everything okay? *Is* everything okay?"

"Yeah, everything's fine."

"I hope I didn't overstep when I came over. I was trying to help."

"I know." I kicked at the polished floor. "No one overstepped. I just didn't..." I paused. "It didn't feel the same, being there with Alice."

"Yeah, I know. I was that way with Juliet. I'm still that way. It's like when you're a kid, and you have your favorite kind of candy clutched in your fist. You know it's polite to share, but you don't want to fucking share, because it's your favorite treat and there's only so much of it." He chuckled, picking up one of the gears he'd taken off earlier. "It was pretty clear to everyone who knew you that you didn't feel like sharing Saturday night."

"I have never, ever felt the way I felt on Saturday night." I moved closer, watching Fort root through his belt for a very small screwdriver. "Alice was worried because she didn't know what went wrong, and I was like, *what went wrong is that I love you too much*." I let out a self-deprecating laugh. "It's new territory for me."

"Maybe so," said Fort after a moment. "But it's good territory. What did Alice say when you told her you loved her?"

"She was happy, but she already knew. She's known for a long time." I shook my head. "I don't know, man. I've come to The Gallery for so long. I've been 'that person' here for so long."

"What person?"

"The heartless sex fiend. The relentless sadist who loves sharing women. She says it's okay for me to change—"

"Of course it's okay." Fort laughed. "Ella the flightphobic scientist is learning to fly an airplane. Devin the playboy is shopping for engagement rings. And I'm getting married—" He made a comical, alarmed sound. "In five months, my friend. I guess the question is, are you okay with changing?"

"Yes." I didn't even have to think about it. "For her, because of her, yes, I'll change. But it sucks, you know, not being able to come here anymore, because I think she was into the atmosphere, and the uniform and everything. She's turning into quite the little maso submissive."

"Not shocking, in your hands." He let out a sigh, hooking his fingers in his toolbelt.

"What's wrong?" I asked.

"Nothing. I'm just thinking... This clock has been broken forever, right?"

I nodded. "Since The Gallery opened."

"And the rules have also been the same since day one." He picked up one of the larger gears, adding it back to the center. "Do you know anything about potential and kinetic energy?"

I frowned up at him. "What the fuck, man?"

"Forget it. Listen. Maybe I'm fixing this clock now because the time for standing still is over. Like Alice told you, it's okay to change. It's okay for me to change, and Dev to change. It's okay for you to change."

"It's just a clock."

Fort took a step back and started pushing the hands from their longtime position at 7:45, to the current time, which was just after noon.

"It would be a simple change, wouldn't it?" he called down to me. "Instead of *Any submissive brought into The Gallery shall be considered communal property blah blah blah*, shorten it to *Any submissive may be shared in any way her sponsor desires*. Strike the part about communal property. It's barely a rule change, just a refinement."

He made it sound simple, but it wasn't. "It'll change everything about The Gallery."

"Will it, though? Some members are into sharing. Some aren't. Some want to share on certain nights, but not others. It's always been a dance of consent. Remember the time Devin attacked you for slapping Ella?"

I grimaced. "Remember the time you glowered at everyone who looked in Juliet's direction? That's why no one tries to play with her anymore."

"Exactly. The practice of discretion has already been going on." I heard a buzzing sound, and Fort flinched and shook out his fingers.

"You okay, man?"

"I'm good." He smiled down at me. "Look at that."

For the first time I could remember, the clock's huge gears turned, and the minute hand inched a tiny degree with every second's *click, click, click*. Fort looked at his watch while I marked the clicks with the stopwatch on my phone. Thirty seconds. A minute. It matched up perfectly.

"Holy shit, Forsyth." I let out a whistle. "You got it working again."

"I told you that piece would solve everything." He climbed down the scaffolding, amazingly nimble for a guy his size. "And there's a piece that'll solve everything for you and Alice also. Make sharing optional. Word the new rule so it's at the sponsor's discretion. That way the men still feel like they're in charge, the women still feel owned and controlled, and couples who don't want to play with other people can do their own thing."

I thought a moment, looking up at the clock. "Maybe. It might work. I'll send an email to the current members, see what they think. I'd love to bring her back here, you know?"

"It's better than Underworld any day," Fort said. "Even if I met my future wife outside that skank hole. I think Juliet and I would come back here more often if you made that small change to the rules."

"What about the collars?" I asked. "They all say '*Property of The Gallery.*'"

"So? Hell, we're all property of The Gallery when you think about it. We're the ones who make this place come alive on Saturday night."

He had a point there, and coming with Alice would make it even more alive for me. I thought of bringing her back in her gorgeous uniform and stockings, letting others look but not touch. That was as sexy as sharing, now that I thought about it.

"No, man, wait." Fort smacked his head. "It's so obvious. The collars, the locks. If a submissive's communal property on any given night, she wears the *Property of The Gallery* lock on her collar. If she's not available to other Doms, no lock. They can come on and off."

"That's genius." And he was right, it was such an obvious solution. "That way, the ones who get off on the communal property thing can still have their fun times—"

"And the couples who aren't so into sharing can have their boundaries respected without a lot of uncomfortable body language."

"And punching, in Dev's case," I joked, rubbing my eye where he'd landed a vicious left. "This is good." I smiled at Fort. "Seriously, it'll be a good change. I think everyone will be on board with it."

"Agreed. Oh, and when you email everyone, make sure you tell them we're keeping proper time now, thanks to me."

I looked at the turning gears, watching them connect for the first time since we'd bought this clock tower. "Where'd you find that missing piece, anyway?"

"I didn't find it, my friend. I made it with my 'petite metal solder' and those fancy jeweler's tools you always make fun of. You're not the only one who can build cool stuff in a workshop."

"How'd you figure out the right size?" I squinted to make out the small inner workings beneath the big gears. "How'd you make it fit?"

"Skill and experience," he laughed, making a lewd finger-in-the-hole gesture. "With enough patience, you can fit anything anywhere. Speaking of workshops, how does Alice like her new violin?"

"She loves it. It gets a name this weekend. We're flying to Italy to see my parents, and, I guess, everyone else she hasn't seen for a while. Her parents are meeting us there too."

"Wow, a big family thing in Milan."

"All Fierro violins officially come from Italy," I said. "Once it has my mother's blessing—and name—it's formally adopted and registered."

"Congrats, man. That's a big deal. The family stuff, more than anything. I don't know. Alice might be the one. If so, you're a lucky man."

"I'm a very lucky man." I couldn't keep the smile off my face. "It's so weird. I never thought everything would work out like this. For me. For you. For Devin."

He studied me a moment, then shook his head, taking off his toolbelt. "Yes, you did. With you and Alice, you knew. It was pretty apparent to us, anyway, from the first time we saw you two together. Maybe we don't deserve the women we ended up with, but I, for one, am not going to let that stop me." He punched me on the shoulder. "Now get out of here and write that email, you selfish motherfucker. It's time for The Gallery, Version Two."

CHAPTER TWENTY:
ALICE

We dropped Blue at Milo's parents' home in Chappaqua, so he could be spoiled by their house staff for the weekend, and run wild across their wide open lawn. I watched in amazement as he broke into a sprint the minute we hit the backyard. He went from lazy dog to rocket streak in the space of a few seconds, kicking up sod with his narrow feet.

"Jesus. I never knew Blue could run like that."

"Of course he can run like that. He was a great racer in his day." Milo smiled at me. "Even though he's changed, he's still got that wildness in him. He likes to let it out now and again."

Blue blew past us with a big dog grin on his face, starting lap two of the fence's perimeter. I squeezed Milo's hand, smiling back. "It's good to know that wildness isn't gone."

We left Westchester County Airport on a private flight to Atlanta, and picked up a transatlantic Gibraltar Air flight from there. Devin wasn't in the cockpit this time. Milo told me his friend sometimes flew that route, but this particular weekend, he was taking Ella to Martha's Vineyard to propose to her, skywriters over the beach and everything.

"That's so perfect," I said. "Ella will love it, because she studies space and stuff."

"Yes, Dev's been working on his proposal speech for a couple weeks. The big line is: *You're my whole universe.*"

I pretended to faint. "That's too romantic. I'm dead."

"Me too. We're both dead."

We slumped in our first class seats together, settling in for the hop over to Milan. The violin he'd made me was in its case, tucked carefully beneath the seat. Skywritten proposals and speeches of love were all well and good, but he'd made me a violin that would last hundreds of years, and bring me, and future owners, untold magnitudes of happiness. When I played Milo's violin, I felt those magnitudes in the tones it produced. He'd made me a miraculous thing.

And yet he could still sit beside me, a normal, slightly frazzled man. "Worried about seeing your family?" I asked.

"Why would I be worried?"

"It's your parents' first time hearing this violin. My parents too."

"Think they won't like it?"

"You know they're going to like it," I said, nudging him. "You're worried that your father will be upset when he realizes you've become a better luthier than him or your grandfather."

"Shh." He shook his head. "Not better or worse, just different." He took my chin in his hands and kissed me, rough and quick. "And if they hear you play it, of course it's going to sound like the finest violin in the history of the world."

"Too romantic. I'm dying again."

He grinned at me as he brushed back an errant lock of his dark hair. As the plane flew over the ocean, I thought about which song I should play for our families as we celebrated Milo's achievement. Probably Vivaldi. There was no better choice to express my happiness. It wasn't great to lose everything you owned in an explosion and fire, but I was alive, and everything had turned out more wonderfully than I could have imagined.

"Oh," said Milo, turning to me. "I was talking to Fort on Monday, about The Gallery and the rules. He suggested we tweak them a little."

"Yeah?"

"Yeah. For those of us who have trouble sharing our pretty toys. You know the lock on the collar, the one that says *Property of the Gallery*?"

"Oh!" I blinked at him. "Members can take them on and off."

He threw up his hands. "If it's so obvious to everyone, why are we only thinking of this now? Yes, the idea is that people who are into sharing have the lock attached, and people who want a private scene leave it off. I explained it in the email to all the current members, and every response so far has been positive, so..."

"So we can go back!"

"Yes, if you want to."

"That's amazing news. Yes, I want to!" My one sadness about loving Milo was that he might have to forgo certain needs on my account. Now, even if he didn't want to share me, he could take me to the dungeon he'd help build, and let out some of that wildness that attracted me in the first place. "Although, if we go back, you might *hurt me there*," I whispered.

"Don't flirt with me. Not now, when I can't do anything about it."

"We'll be in Milan in a few hours, if you really want to do something about it."

"You realize we won't be in the same room, right? Knowing my mother, once she finds out we're a couple, she'll make you bed down in a whole different wing of the house."

"Then I'll sneak over to your wing after dark. I'm not afraid of your mother." I thought a moment. "Actually, I am a little afraid of your mother. Do you know the name she decided on? The one she picked for my violin?"

"She might not know it herself yet. She'll want to pick it up first and see what it's 'telling her.' All Fierro matriarchs possess special violin-communicating abilities." His fingers tightened on mine, and he gave me a look that made my heart pound wildly in my chest. "Maybe you'll be the next one, Alice. You're pretty good with violins, even if you're not Italian."

All I could do was stare at him. So many things flashed through my mind: music, children, a happy marriage, and waking up next to Milo every day, kissing him good morning and running my fingers through his tousled, bedhead hair. "I'll sully the Fierro family line with my ginger-Swedish genes," I joked, to cover my deeper feelings. "Maybe we're not a good idea after all."

"There are ginger Italians too. It's possible you're stuck with me, Lala. We'll see."

Our relationship was young, with plenty of years to develop, but it also felt old as time, especially when he called me Lala. I closed my eyes and rested my head against his shoulder, dreaming of Italian weddings and spirited ginger-Milo babies. In a way, I couldn't picture any of it, because the dream was too wonderful and gigantic, but in another way, it felt like it'd always been meant to be.

* * * * *

We'd flown through rays of sunshine when we left Atlanta, but we landed in Milan under a pall of dark clouds. The Italian skies poured down summer rain, so we had to stow the violin case in a protective plastic pouch before we left the terminal. Even with umbrellas, and a car to pick us up, we arrived at Casa di Fierro in uncomfortably wet clothes. Milo's parents welcomed us at the door, and my parents emerged from the kitchen, passing around hugs even though we were soaked.

Then our parents all stood back and looked at us, and I thought, *they know. They see it. They know we're in love with each other.* Luciana Fierro wore a huge smile, but no one made us profess our feelings after all these years.

Milo went to change in his childhood room, and I was shown to my guest room, not in a different wing, but definitely at the opposite end of the hallway. My parents' room adjoined mine, and we spent time catching up on news in overlapping Swedish while I changed and unpacked. My mother worked the conversation around to Milo as soon as she could.

"Will you stay at his place through the summer?" she asked. "Are you still looking for apartments?"

"Well, kind of," I said. "But not really."

"I told you, Freja," said my father, laughing. "She'll move in with him, but she'll never move out."

"Is there a romance between you, finally?" My mother's voice went soft when she was excited. "Have you fallen in love?"

"Yes, I think so." I grinned, accepting their ecstatic hugs. "But you can't tell Milo's parents. You know how they are about cohabitation before marriage and all that." My Swedish parents were considerably more lax on the issue. Only my impending birth had nudged them into the registrar's office for an official marriage certificate.

My mother held me, squeezing me in her arms. "My sweet girl. We wondered how long it would take both of you to realize that you ought to be in love."

"Well, I'll tell you, it took a bunch of arguments and misunderstandings, but it also took no time at all."

"Will the wedding be in Italy or Sweden?" my father asked. "Sweden, I hope."

"New York," my mother said. "To keep the peace."

"Don't say anything about it to anyone," I pleaded. "Everything's very new. There may not be a wedding. Maybe we'll break up next week."

"Maybe," said my father. "One never knows." But his stern blond brows waggled, expressing disbelief and making me laugh.

An hour later, we sat to eat a late Italian lunch on the covered *terrazza*. The sun had finally emerged, with birds chirping and flitting outside the screen as we enjoyed fresh bread, salads, lemon-braised fish, and wine. I wondered if Milo had gotten the same probing questions from his parents as I did. He was smiling beside me, but still tense. The violin sat at the end of the table, propped on its case, overseeing the proceedings.

At the end of the meal, when the dishes were cleared away, Milo's father brought more wine, and his mother took the violin in her hands, turning it over with careful scrutiny.

"O, *mio figlio*," she sighed. "It's a beautiful violin." Her sparkling eyes fixed on me. "You've played it already, no?"

"Many times. But not in public," I added. "I was waiting for the name."

"I have a name," she said in her thick accent. She turned it over, her finger tracing over the tiny, camouflaged heart as if it was an obvious feature. "We'll call it the Heartsong, for this heart, and the one that came before it."

Milo's eyes darted toward his father. The older man smiled. "Yes, I saw it. You think I didn't? I let it go, since, somehow, it improved the violin's tone."

Tears welled in my eyes. The Heartsong. It was an unusually emotional choice for a top-flight instrument. Now the heart, *our* heart, would be a named feature of the violin. Eyes would seek it out in the grain, and fingers would trace it for many years to come. "I love it," I said. "I love that name." I met Luciana's eyes as she handed it across the table to me, and some of the tears spilled over. My mom gave a loud sniff, and my dad suddenly became very interested in his napkin.

Milo handed me his napkin so I could wipe my eyes, since mine had disappeared. "I thought I hid the heart so well," he said.

"You can't hide your heart from those who see it," his mother said in a soft scold. "Once they know it's there."

I've always seen your heart, I thought. *I've always known it was there.* When I met his dark, fond gaze, all the tears I'd wiped away started overflowing again. "I'm so grateful for this," I said to him. "I can never explain how much... Well, I'm going to treasure this." I took a shaky breath. "My Heartsong violin."

"I'm glad you like the name," he said. Then, in front of everyone, he tilted up my chin and kissed the tears on my cheeks. Time seemed to stand still as he leaned closer and kissed my lips, a slow, lingering, but mostly chaste kiss. "I love you," he whispered, just for me, then he turned to our parents and said, "I love her. I've always loved her, but now I..." He paused and fixed his gaze back on mine. "Now I *really* love her. And Ma..." He stood to go to her. "You picked the perfect name. Thank you."

My mom was openly sobbing now, and Luciana wiped her eyes, rising to give Milo a kiss on both cheeks. I was next, and afterward she took my face between her hands and looked at me with unfettered glee. "I knew you two would end up together. A mother knows the woman who deserves her son's heart. When you're ready, we can start thinking about the wedding. Until then, maybe you can move to our house in Chappaqua. We have plenty of room."

"Ma," Milo protested.

"That would be best, no?" she said, ignoring his complaint.

"It's fine for her to stay with me. She sleeps in the guest room."

Luciana shook a finger at her son. "I know you better than that."

"I think Alice can decide where she wants to stay. She's an adult."

"These are matters to discuss later," Milo's father interrupted. He nodded at the newly christened violin, still clutched in my fingers. "Let's hear it played. Let's hear this Heartsong violin, and see if it lives up to its name."

The others around the table agreed, cheering and clapping. I stood beside Milo, composing myself, bringing the violin to rest beneath my chin, where it had already come to feel natural and right. Milo handed over the bow from my case. I played a few long, slow notes to show off the instrument's resonance, then launched into Vivaldi's *Violin Concerto in G major.*

Luciana clapped her hands, delighted. Heads nodded as my fingers flew through the rollicking notes and my bow tipped back and forth across the strings. This had been one of my first recital pieces—in a simpler version, of course—and still a song that brought instant joy to my heart. My heartsong, played on my Heartsong, which had been given to me by my heart's own dream. The notes I loved sounded brighter and clearer than they'd ever sounded before.

Later that night, I crept down the hall to Milo's room and let myself in, turning to close the door without making a sound. Before I could finish, I was grabbed, a hand pressed over my mouth to muffle the instinctive scream.

Milo. I love you. When he felt me relax, he closed the door himself.

"Did anyone see you?" he whispered.

I shook my head, and his hand moved from my mouth to circle my neck. I let out a slow breath, pressing my back along his front.

"I need you," he said, pulling me with him toward the bed. "I've had Vivaldi in my head all day. I need to be inside you."

"I'm here. I'm yours."

As I lay back and welcomed him on top of me, I knew things would get scary, that he'd take me a little further into his world before he let me return to my safe guest room bed. I knew I'd end up bound, bitten, choked, and probably sore, since the only way he could hurt me would be with things that were quiet. When he produced rope from his bag, and a small, very silent whip, I held out my wrists in surrender.

Play me, Milo. Let me be your Heartsong, and play me with joy.

THE END

A Final Note

I hope you enjoyed this final book in my Dark Dominance series. After Fort's theme of energy (*Dark Control*) and Devin's theme of space (*Deep Control*), I wanted to make Milo's story about time, and his relationship with Alice that deepened over so many years. We long for things, and sometimes we're able to get them. Sometimes we settle. Sometimes we give up, but when we get the things we long for, it brings such vast amounts of joy. I wanted brooding, passionate Milo to find joy in the end, along with his friends, but for him, I wanted it to be a painful, drawn-out journey. What else does a sadist like him deserve? It makes his and Alice's happily ever after that much sweeter in my mind.

Many thanks to the posse of helpers who made this book, and this series, possible. Josie Kerr, Tiffany, Carol, Wendy, Nina and Chanpreet of Social Butterfly PR, and all my Club Annabel Facebook crew. Thanks also to the wonderful readers who write to me, review my books online, and otherwise provide kind and generous encouragement. You're my joy; I couldn't do this without you.

You may also enjoy
these BDSM romances by Annabel Joseph

Owning Wednesday

OWNING WEDNESDAY is an emotionally charged romance about being scared, being owned, and being loved.

Wednesday is released by Vincent, her long-time Master, only to find herself in a new, much more intense power exchange relationship with Daniel. But is Vincent really out of her life forever? Can Wednesday bear the intimacy of her new lover's demands?

The three soon find themselves in an uneasy and sometimes downright contentious love triangle. Wednesday wants to submit to Daniel, but self-protective impulses and bad memories make their budding relationship a constant struggle. In a world of passion, promises, and power exchange, Wednesday and her lovers must come to understand the difference between being "owned" and loved.

Firebird

Prosper is thrilled to be plucked from the corps de ballet to dance the lead role in Firebird. But Jackson, the guest choreographer, is as sexy as he is demanding. Prosper soon finds herself flustered by his closeness and his unforgiving gaze. She gets caught up in kinky fantasies that make it difficult for her to concentrate on his steps. She imagines him as her Dominant, turning her over his knee for flubs in rehearsal. Just as sensual tension at work builds to an impossible level, a surprise encounter outside the studio results in Prosper's fantasies being realized. Jackson takes his protégée home and ties her to his bed. Soon Prosper is receiving the discipline and domination she craves—and much, much more.

The pair maintain a secret off-stage relationship—scorchingly intimate encounters several evenings a week. But Prosper feels the burden of carrying the Firebird ballet on her back, and Jackson knows that his time in New York will draw to an end all too soon. Will Prosper crack under the pressure of pleasing her lover and bringing his vision to life, or will Jackson find a way to help his Firebird take flight?

THE IRONCLAD BODYGUARD SERIES BY ANNABEL JOSEPH, WRITING AS MOLLY JOSEPH

PAWN: High stakes chess competition has always been a man's game—until Grace Ann Frasier topples some of the game's greatest champions and turns the chess world on its ear. Her prowess at the game is matched only by her rivals' desire to defeat her, or, worse, avenge their losses. When an international championship threatens Grace's safety, a bevy of security experts are hired to look after her, but only one is her personal, close-duty bodyguard, courtesy of Ironclad Solutions, Inc.

Sam Knight knows nothing about chess, but he knows Grace is working to achieve something important, and he vows to shelter her from those who mean her harm. When she leans on him for emotional support, attraction battles with professionalism and Sam finds his self-discipline wavering. Soon the complexity of their relationship resembles a chess board, where one questionable move can ruin everything—or win a game that could resonate around the world.

DIVA: In his years at Ironclad, Ransom has built a reputation as a hardass bodyguard. He reels in the perverts, wrangles the mangled, and controls celebrities who are notoriously out of control.

So when a world-famous DJ starts slipping into risky habits, he's hired to keep her on track during a multi-million-dollar tour. He figures he'll just knock the diva down a few pegs and scare her straight. Problem is, Lola isn't easily frightened, and "difficult" doesn't begin to describe their contentious relationship. The only thing more annoying than their daily fights and power struggles is their intensifying emotional connection.

Ransom's determined to save her...even if she doesn't want to be saved.

Exclusive Paperback Bonus:

Thirty Favorite Scenes from Thirty Annabel Joseph Novels

Now that she's reached her ten-year publishing anniversary, Annabel Joseph looks back over her library of thirty BDSM novels to share the scenes that stuck with her the most. Caution: spoilers!

Club Mephisto: It's hard to pick a favorite scene from this book, because there were so many scenes that felt powerful when I was writing them. But if I had to narrow it down, I'd say it was the scene at the end of "The Seventh Day" when her Master shows up to take her home and Molly bursts into happy tears. She's been so changed over the week, so challenged, but as soon as she sees her Master, none of that matters as much as the fact that he's there to embrace her. I guess it's disappointing that I didn't pick one of the super hardcore sex scenes. I mean, I love those too, but that scene where her Master returns really underlines the whole essence of Molly, that she is absolutely surrendered and absolutely in love with him, no matter what kind of trials she has to endure.

Molly's Lips: Club Mephisto Retold: I think my favorite part of this book is "The Sixth Day," particularly the first few paragraphs, when Mephisto worries that he might have killed Molly from the orgasm denial regimen (haha). But the whole chapter's a fascinating look at him, because his inner dialogue shows a lot of his unease and frustration with the Molly situation. All week he's been her stern, inflexible trainer and Master, but we see now that there are a lot of times he's not sure if he's doing the right thing for her, or whether he understands her at all. Molly thinks D-types in the lifestyle know everything, and are infallible. A really fun part of telling the story from Mephisto's point of view is that we get to see him, and even Clayton, struggling with the challenges of being a worthy, conscientious Master. When you're dealing with Molly's kind of super-deep submission, it's not an easy thing.

Burn For You: Okay, I'll mention the obvious one, which is the scene near the end when Molly visits the cemetery with her violin and her child to update Clayton on her life. I bawled my eyes out when I wrote it, every time I edited it, and every time I read it to this day. But there are two other scenes, similar in nature, that I enjoy going back to read because they're super angsty. The first is when Mephisto gives Molly a ride home after her Master's burial, and she denounces everything she and Clayton had together, and expresses shame at being a slave for so long. Mephisto's horrified, and I was horrified too when the plot veered that way, because Molly was so pure in the first two books, and here she was doubting, even despising her old Master. As we read it, we're just like Mephisto: *You're wrong, Molly. No!* The other scene I love is when Mephisto visits Lorna at the beginning of Chapter Thirteen. In a way they're related scenes because there's more doubting. Lorna doubts that Mephisto knows what he's doing. She doubts that Molly should become a mother, or that Mephisto should have gotten involved with her at all. But in our hearts, as readers, we know that Molly and Mephisto love and need each other. Through all the angst and doubt, they finish strong and earn that happily ever after. (And Lorna comes around too.)

Deep in the Woods: There's a sequence I especially love at the start of Chapter Seven, when Dave's in the dark room printing the pictures he took of Sophie at the park. I dated a couple of photographers during my college years, back in the day when dark rooms and chemical photo development was still a thing, and they'd both taken me into the dark room with them at different points. Watching them create the photos from film and chemicals seemed like such a magical, mystery-laden thing. I was still in touch with one of my photography exes, so I asked him to walk me through the process so I could recreate it in the story. There's some metaphor there, with how carefully he adjusts the chemicals and the exposure to get the best picture, and how carefully he adjusts his interactions with Sophie because of the abuse she suffered.

Fortune: This one's a tie. My first favorite scene is near the start of Chapter Two, when Kat wakes up in the hospital and sees the origami figures, and then finds "Dr. Ryan" standing at the end of her bed.

"So you really are a doctor."

"I don't lie, Ekaterina. Ever. Yes, I am a doctor."

I love the awkwardness of everything that happens between them in the hospital, including Mama Elena's overbearing presence.

My second favorite scene is the one where he first ties Kat up, and demonstrates his love of shibari. He makes her crawl around while she's bound and pick up origami cranes in her mouth, which isn't just an exercise in housekeeping. There's so much in that scene about power and submission, and the deep feelings it can bring. I wrote this book early in my career, and it has so many personal connections to me, and so many themes that came together in just the right way. Sometimes I wish I'd written it later along the line, so I would have had the talent and experience to make it just a bit more polished, but I also kind of enjoy the reckless pathos of *Fortune*. It's a very emotional book.

Cait and the Devil: Oh goodness, speaking of reckless early writing... I remember someone reviewing this book alongside my other books and dismissing it as "just silly," and CATD is silly in many ways, but it's probably one of my most creative books, in that I brought in the fantasy elements, the medieval kingdom, kings and priestesses, and even a little humor with Cait's innocence. I think my favorite scene is in Chapter Four, when she's in the apple tree refusing to come down. It's the first scene where Duncan realizes he's developing deeper feelings for her. It's also the first time he spanks her—but he also promises to hold her afterward. Aww. I loved this scene so much that the original cover for *Cait and the Devil* had an apple tree illustration on the front. I had to change it since it didn't scream "romance," but there's definitely a lot of metaphor there. The apples, temptation, the way she hovers above him like the angel she is... It was a scene I wrote many times through my adolescence and young adulthood, and it ended up in final form in this book.

Comfort Object: Okay, it's going to be almost impossible to pick a favorite from this book. This is another early book that's so blunt and so recklessly emotional. I was going through my own emotional upheavals at the time, and nursing a real crush on an actor who I pictured as Jeremy Gray in my mind, and somehow that all congealed into this seething morass of violence, longing, and sexuality on the page. I guess my favorite scene has to be that penultimate breakdown when Jeremy's feelings grow so unmanageable that he burns all of Nell's beloved mythology books. That's the scene readers mention to me the most. (*I couldn't believe he did that. I hated him!*) Every so often I like to write a scene where the hero is such an asshole we're not sure we can ever forgive him. That was definitely one of those scenes.

Caressa's Knees: *Comfort Object* was originally supposed to be a standalone story, but readers kept asking me, "where's Kyle's story?" I was like, *What? Kyle is just a secondary character.* But so many readers fell in love with his protective nature and his selflessness that I decided after a few years to write a story for him too, and the rest of the Comfort series developed from there. My favorite scene happens when he takes Caressa to Spur, Texas to get her out of her head, and show her what life is like outside her self-imposed musical prison. The scene at Burger's Pond with the fireflies is about recognizing the wonder that's all around us, if we'd just take the time to breathe and to look. Caressa gets choked up, because she's realizing everything she's missing due to her musical obsession and guilt, and how much more beautiful her life could be. There's this moment where Kyle gives her one of the fireflies to hold in her hand, and he says, "Careful. Hold it loosely. Don't crush it." And she thinks the firefly got away, but then it lights up in her hand, and she's like, *omg, wow.* To me, that tiny moment is like a metaphor for how we love. Then he teaches her to swim, to *float*, and that whole scene becomes one huge love fest in my mind.

Odalisque: Constance was the first heroine I wrote with a disability. Someone close to me has a hearing loss, and I thought, what an interesting challenge for a character in a power exchange relationship— she can't hear, so her partner has to show what he wants, and she has to be that much more attuned to his desires. I had fun showing all that Constance could do, even with her hearing loss. I also had a lot of fun exploring the whole "Odalisque" kink, which is a real-life thing. But if I had to pick my favorite scene, I'd pick the scene in the grotto midway through Chapter Five. I like it because it's the beginning of their attempt to communicate, and deliciously awkward in that way, and I like it because it's when Kai chooses her, which brings her a lot of joy. I also like the sensuality of this beautiful, private pool, and the entomology vs. etymology joke, which amused me very much. For the record, this scene is also a fave because it's an homage to one of my favorite scenes in Laura Kinsale's historical romance *Shadowheart*, where the hero and heroine have quite a scene in a similar grotto. If you haven't read Laura Kinsale, just read all of them. They're all amazing.

Command Performance: Ah, Mason was such a fun character to write. Satya was fun as a supporting character, and Miri was a fun heroine because she was so virginal and horny. I had so much fun finishing the Comfort series with this book, even though Mason and Miri had some hard times on their way to happily ever after. I adore the scene in the limo after the Golden Globes, when Mason's all ready to make out with her and realizes she's never been kissed before, and takes all that trauma to Satya, whose response cracks me up. There's something about Mason being this grown up, hyper masculine, crazy little man-boy who wants to do things the right way, but mainly flails around. But my favorite guilty pleasure in that book is the scene in Chapter Seventeen when Mason goes to Miri's house and realizes for the first time that she's carrying his baby. Maybe it's not realistic, but their argument is a riot, and then Peter stabs Mason and it just becomes this over the top scene that's so perfect for a hero like Mason Cooke. Miri yells, "Daddy, are you crazy?" and Mason answers, "Yes, he's crazy, he fucking stabbed me in the shoulder!" So awesome. Good times.

Disciplining the Duchess: I have about eleventy hundred favorite scenes in this book. Let's see if I can narrow it down, because I really put a lot of my long time fantasies and awkward situations in here, with the stern duke and the rapscallion young miss. The most delicious scene to me is probably the second part of Chapter Six, called "Wonder," when Court takes Harmony to the Roman ruins and watches this woman, whom he knows he's going to have to marry, wander around these old ruins and ruminate about all kinds of wonderful things. The capper is when she makes him lie down so he can "feel the earth moving under them." He feels ridiculous and he's sure he'd never do such a thing, but then he does, for her. All the while, she has no idea that she's going to have to marry this stern duke, because she thinks no one would press such an uneven match. You can tell that was one of my fave scenes because I did a "mirror" scene in the epilogue, when they return to the Roman ruins and lie back on the earth again with their lovely children frolicking around them.

Waking Kiss: This wins the award for hardest book to write. Oh, how I wrote and re-wrote this, and agonized over it, and cried. Not only did the main characters not cooperate with what I wanted them to do; there was also Rubio, who was supposed to be a stock-character baddie, and ended up stealing my heart. Two of my favorite things about this book were Ashleigh's blanket fort, and the Sleeping Beauty bed of branches, both of which stood metaphorically for the ways Liam and Ashleigh hid from one another, and also kept each other safe. But if we're talking about my personal favorite scene, I have to be honest and say it's in the first chapter, when Ashleigh has to dance with The Great Rubio in her disastrously noisy toe shoes. I laugh, I cry, I feel so bad for her, and Rubio is such an asshole. It's just a funny, traumatic scene.

Fever Dream: I do love the scene where Rubio and Petra meet, and he calls her a "big-forehead robot." Oh Ruby, what a mess you are. He provides a lot of comic relief in a story that's kind of stressful with Petra's stalker running around. Then there's the Rubio-Petra-Liam ménage in the rightfully famous Chapter Sixteen. But I think my favorite scene is in Chapter Eighteen, when Rubio and Petra run into Petr Grigolyuk in the corridor. Now Grigolyuk IS a super baddie, the worst kind of baddie, and when Rubio confronts him on Petra's behalf, it's so satisfying. Forget the fact that Rubio and Petra have been feuding, and that they're definitely "professional only" at that moment. Rubio still rips into Grigolyuk and says all the things that need to be said, because no matter how flighty and rude and self-centered he is, he loves Petra. There's a little line that ends that section: *His expression looked as savage as his heart was pure.* That's Rubio when it all comes down to it, which is why I adore him so much.

Lily Mine: This was my first attempt at combining Regency-ish era romance with kink and spanking, and I remember having a pretty hard time with it. As opposed to my later historical series, like Properly Spanked, *Lily Mine* has a calmer, more regimented feel to the spanking scenes, I guess because it was more a fetish for Lord Ashbourne than a way to control a wayward, naughty wife. I find the sex and spanking scenes kind of fascinating to read back over for that reason. One of the most interesting and lovely scenes for me is the second part of Chapter Seven, when Lily is "caught" perving Lord Ashbourne's pornographic stash in the attic. He toys with her a little, makes her obey his commands, and soon they're reenacting her favorite scenes from his books. There's a great line at the end of the interlude about "no more shame between us" that really opens up their kinky relationship and desire for one another. I found it a lot easier to finish writing the book after that scene.

Mercy: This was the first book I wrote, kind of concurrently with *Owning Wednesday*. It's so raw that it's kind of painful for me to read now. I think everyone wants me to write "another *Mercy*" but this was at such a particular time in my life, and it was the first time I allowed myself to pour out these angsty fantasies. I'm not sure I could reproduce something like that again, because I've tried. (The last attempt turned into *Waking Kiss*, so…) With that said, my favorite scene is Chapter Eleven, after the awful, confusing night at Frank and Byron's dungeon, when Lucy finally safe words with Matthew. He comes to get her and soothe her (a little late on aftercare, crazy man) and he explains the "reality" of everything that had been going on the night before. At the time I wrote this, I was really struggling with that line between what's real and what's fantasy in BDSM, and where that line should be. Then there's the rest of the chapter, when Matthew insists he's not in love with her (ha!) and then Frank and Byron show up to make a play for Lucy at the stage door. That's when things start to really come apart, so I like it. It's a great pivotal scene in a book that, in hindsight, probably isn't that skillfully organized or executed. But hey, all the *feelings* are there in spades.

Owning Wednesday: Besides being one of my first two books, this also has two different versions. The first one was overblown with backstory and Wednesday's inner dialogue. When Loose Id republished it, they (rightly) requested that I scale that back, so while the final version was sleeker, it almost feels too spare to me, because so much of the original was cut out. I guess it taught me a good lesson on finding balance. Whether bloated or spare, my favorite scene in OW remains the same. It's the scene at the end of Chapter Twelve, when Wednesday confronts Vincent and insists on learning whether he ever loved her. Vincent has this line, "Could I have given you up any other way?" The love story is essentially Daniel and Wednesday's, but Vincent was a big part of helping them find each other. This dynamic of the older Master guiding and ultimately giving up a beloved submissive was repeated in the Mephisto series.

Cirque de Minuit: I loved Cirque du Soleil long before I decided to write books based in a similar setting. Who would have thought the Cirque books would turn out as filthy and heartfelt as they did? Theo started the whole thing, because he was so filthy and yet so heartfelt. My favorite scene is the one where he takes Kelsey out to the woods and teaches her to go "flying" on the silks for the first time. *Afraid, girl?* In that scene, he's this wonderful combination of protective, taunting, and flirtatious. Then there's the scene that immediately follows, where they "christen" the silks. Ooh la la! Runner up fave scene: the surprise, quasi-consensual butt sex in Chapter Six.

Bound in Blue: My goodness, Jason turned out to be so much more hardcore in this book than I expected. I love all the scenes between Jason and Sara, because they were such a great kink match, but my favorite scene in the book is probably the start of Chapter Six, when Lemaitre shows up in a panic about Sara missing, and then has his little "talking to" with Jason about sleeping with her. Then she comes out of the bedroom and (spoiler, spoiler, spoiler) at that point I knew as a writer that he was meeting his adult daughter for the first time, but Jason and Sara didn't know, and the reader doesn't know either, not yet. I loved the way Sara stood up to his scolding, because you know in Lemaitre's head, he's like, *"that's my girl."* I had so much fun setting up the plot development for this book. I was really proud of myself.

Master's Flame: I worked myself into a panic about writing a book that was "good enough" for the legend that was Le Maitre, but *Master's Flame* was easier to write than I thought. I think it's because Valentina was such a lively character. Between the two of them, sparks were flying all over the place with very little effort on my part. There are so many hot, hot scenes I love, but I think my favorite is in Chapter Six, when he finally agrees to become her Master, and she signs a contract on black ink on the wall: *I belong to Le Maitre.* Minutes later, he's shoving his huge cock in her ass, and when she protests, he moves her so he can fuck her against the wall while she stares at the contract she just signed. So evil. So hurty. So heartless. Of course, all ends well. He tames her, but she tames him too, which is kind of fun when he started out as such a scary beast.

Firebird: Also known as the not-as-terrifying ballet book. Jackson has his moments as a Dom, but overall his dominance is less scary than Matthew's, and the real romance here is the ballet Jackson and Prosper create together at the same time they're working out a BDSM relationship. There's something so sexy about collaboration, especially when emotions are running strong. I'd say my favorite scene in *Firebird* is the one in Chapter Thirteen when she's trying to do the lift with Blake, and Jackson's like, *Be brave, just do it,* but it's so hard for her run and throw herself into her partner's arms because she's afraid of getting hurt. Of course, it's a metaphor for all her doubts about herself, and about love. It connects to the final lines, when she and Jackson have found love, the ballet is launched, and the lift works perfectly: *She felt herself buoyed by hope, soaring with happiness.*
Like magic, she flew.

Training Lady Townsend: By the time I got to this series, I was much more experienced in writing historical kink. That's the excuse I use for why this series turned out so, so naughty. More than a few readers have been shocked. (Pleasantly, one hopes.) My favorite scene in TLT is the grasshopper scene in Chapter Nine. There's the metaphor of confinement and freedom, of course, but the grasshopper scene is also the first scene where Aurelia doesn't "my lord" him, and where they have a sweet, fun time together instead of spankings, lectures, and dread. I loved that he called her a grasshopper at the start of their relationship, because she jumped whenever he touched her, and chirped in dismay, and it becomes a sweet nickname by the end of the book. This is really a story about turning lemons into some very sweet lemonade.

To Tame a Countess: After Aurelia was such a proper English rose, I wanted a wilder heroine in the second book. Of course, rakish Lord Warren would need someone a little outside the norm, and Josephine fit the bill nicely. My favorite scene is the one near the beginning, when Josephine is running away and Warren comes across her in the woods. The wild animal/tiger metaphor is partly at play. He's certainly stalking her once he comes across her all alone, and convinces her that she must take a spanking from him in order to set things right. He knows he's a scallywag, but he can't help himself. I love the scene after that all the more, because he does the honorable thing and immediately asks to marry her when Lord Baxter finds the two of them alone in the woods. It's that dichotomy of good man vs. rake that makes Regency romance such catnip to me.

My Naughty Minette: This whole book came about because when I was in the planning stages for the series, my friend Tiffany said, "One of them has to sleep with the other one's sister." And she was so right. Minette was a super fun character in all the books, but in her own book, she was such a pleasure to create. The best part is that she'd been in love for so long with the dark, brooding August, who couldn't be more different from her. I love and adore the scene when Warren and the other friends come barging into August's room and find Minette in bed with him, and a virgin's blood on the sheets. How shocking. How squirmy. *How the hell did this happen?* I love how the ensuing marriage pits Warren against August after all their years of friendship. But I think the scene I love most is the scene at the piano after August's father finally dies, and Minette gives him the handkerchief with the "M" on it, and he tells her it's his favorite gift ever, and confides everything to her. It's such a dark, sad scene, but I couldn't wait to write it, and allow August to get all that emotion out.

Under a Duke's Hand: The final book in a series is always a stress bomb, but it's also so satisfying to write. I'd built up such a dignified, confident personality for Arlington, so I knew he needed a woman who would challenge that. I decided on a fiery Welsh lass. I love Chapter Eight, when Gwen runs off on the horse, and Arlington punishes her with a good, hard fucking right there in the clearing where he caught up to her. For once, he loses grip on his iron control. But I can't talk about favorites in this book without talking about the Epilogue, which shows all the couples together in the future, with all their kids playing in the Arlington garden. After spending four books with these couples, that was such fun to imagine and write.

Torment Me: I have no idea where this series came from. It started from the idea of a guy named "W" who was super secretive about his kink and also into poetry, and it went crazy from there. I hate to admit it, because this scene is so not-okay, but my fave section in this book is at the Empire Hotel, when he pretends he's a stranger and forces himself on Chere while she's panicking. I know, I know. It's awful. I also love the scene right after that, where he grovels his way back into her good graces in the rooftop pool. Well, grovels as much as a man like W can grovel. Let's all agree he struggles with some personality flaws.

Taunt Me: I love this book, because Chere—and the readers—finally learn W's real name, what he does for a job, and where he lives. Writing one long story over three books was a new thing for me, and I couldn't freaking wait for this reveal. When he shows back up in her life after two and a half years, the first thing she yells at him is *Tell me your fucking name.* That's my favorite scene, the reunion scene and all the fighting that accompanies it, and then of course, the next thing he does is accuse her of fucking someone else, then he fucks her himself. Only then does he tell her his real name, in the middle of a pretty crazy anal scene. Damn, I had so much fun writing this series.

Trust Me: I love Vinod in this book, and Jino, and Andrew's protectiveness of Chere, and so many things, but my favorite scene is definitely at the end of Chapter Sixteen, when Chere sees the poem Price wrote for her on the mirror at the Gramercy when they finally work out their shit. This series was so much about poetry, and Price not being able to express himself, but he used those three tubes of lipstick to express his feelings for her in a big way. They went through a lot to get to that place.

Dark Control: I'm going to come clean about this. I love this book, I think it's mega hot, and Juliet and Fort make a great couple, but all my favorite parts of this book were the Goodluck scenes. The scene where he talks about his disdain for watches and then wanders out of the Sinclair Jewelry meeting is so funny to me. Of course, time becomes a big theme later on in *Dangerous Control*. If I had to pick one scene between Fort and Juliet that was my favorite, it would be the conversation in his office when he teaches her about potential and kinetic energy using the pendulums. I'm a real nerd for intelligent guys, especially guys who wrap up the lesson on energy by taking you into their home dungeon for a super hot scene.

Deep Control: Ah, I wrote my first STEM heroine with Dr. Ella Novatny. Even as a science-phobe, I had so much fun researching space, astrophysics, and gravitational waves for this book so I could make all those "deep" metaphors work. But my favorite scene isn't a science one, it's the one where Devin has to take over from Captain Ross to crash land the plane in the Azores. I watched a bunch of cockpit videos and read about real-life emergency landings so I could write the scene through to the end with a modicum of accuracy. That scene really got my heart beating, even though I knew things would end well. Runner-up favorite scene: Chapter Seven, blowjob and anal in the shower.

Dangerous Control: This was another one of those series-ending books that was both fun and excruciating to write. I wanted to do Milo Fierro justice, because he was such a mysterious, intense character in the first two books, but I also wanted to get his heart across, and his artistic side. Music was the perfect way to let him express himself, and the perfect way for Alice to see into his heart. The Heartsong thing came to life, and I was happy with how that all turned out. My favorite scene would have to be the scene when he asks her to play the violin in his workshop so he can "take measurements," and they end up playing together. *Sweeping glissandos, trembling vibrato battling for the most perfect resonance...* Of course, that scene wasn't really about them playing music. As always, the metaphor was about love.

To learn more about any of these books, visit your favorite ebook retailer, or check out Annabel's website at annabeljoseph.com.

About the Author

Annabel Joseph is a NYT and USA Today Bestselling BDSM romance author. She writes mainly contemporary romance, although she has been known to dabble in the medieval and Regency eras. She is known for writing emotionally intense BDSM storylines, and strives to create characters that seem real—even flawed—so readers are better able to relate to them. Annabel also writes non-BDSM romance under the pen name Molly Joseph.

You can follow Annabel on Twitter (@annabeljoseph) or Facebook (facebook.com/annabeljosephnovels), or sign up for her mailing list at annabeljoseph.com.

Made in the USA
Middletown, DE
11 July 2024

57199451R00117